To those two Southerners Tom & Janet

INSIDE THE CORTEX

J. M. Graham

with Best Wishes & don't forget to find the Thornborough Eccles
John M. Graham

MINERVA PRESS
MONTREUX LONDON WASHINGTON

INSIDE THE CORTEX
Copyright © J. M. Graham 1996

All Rights Reserved

No part of this book may be reproduced in any form,
by photocopying or by any electronic or mechanical means,
including information storage or retrieval systems,
without permission in writing from both the copyright owner
and the publisher of this book.

ISBN 1 85863 910 7

First Published 1996 by
MINERVA PRESS
195 Knightsbridge
London SW7 1RE

Printed in Great Britain by
B.W.D. Ltd, Northolt, Middlesex.

INSIDE THE CORTEX

Cortex: the outer grey matter of the brain

Oxford English Dictionary

Preface

In an age becoming more and more familiar with computers and microprocessors, the most familiar computer of all is the human brain. It is, however, a computer that is vastly underused and not understood at all. Within the brain is a complex matrix of highways and paths, of hidden information storage areas, of computing devices, and of creative abilities. Only God – if he exists – knows what goes on there in the depths of our sub-brain. But is it normal that we shouldn't be aware of what happens there, of what latent powers lie waiting to be initiated or resurrected? Perhaps the time will come and in that not too distant future when these paths and talents will be investigated, when the layers of the subconscious – the caverns of the mind – will be opened to the light of day for examination.

This story is about one man who does that. You might call it science fiction! But is it? Are our beliefs in too much of a straightjacket of convention, propped up by the scaffolding of the years. Stand in a field one dark night. Pick a soft spring night in the countryside, with a clear dark sky, spotted with millions of pinpricks of light. Look to those heavens and feel the immensity and peace of the universe enclose and lift your spirit. Man's destiny is not to be on this planet. Can't you feel yourself, the very essence of you that is YOU, drawn out there by some power – The Universal Energy – God?

J. M. Graham

This book was grown from a seed of an idea planted by Peter Atkinson. Like a godfather, he watched over it, criticising, advising, and guiding it through its early life. I hope he is satisfied with the final result.

*

The places in this book do exist, more or less as described. Some of the characters do too – in a way. None of them, however, are any single person.

Contents

	The Mystic Depths of the Brain	9
One	The Lecture	11
Two	An Experience at Fountains Abbey	14
Three	The Temple of Mithras	24
Four	Meeting with the professor	35
Five	Another Meeting – at Rievaulx Abbey	46
Six	Post-Mortem	54
Seven	Kate	65
Eight	Meditation	75
Nine	Communication	86
Ten	A Further Advance via Mount Grace	95
Eleven	The Thornborough Circles	109
Twelve	The Gods	121
Thirteen	Joined in Mind	134
Fourteen	Northallerton Church	145
Fifteen	Iona	159
Sixteen	The Final Communion	173
Seventeen	Postscript	184

The Mystic Depths of the Brain

Somewhere, somewhere is the key.

The Key to open the dark forbidding door.

Who lost it?

No one knows.

For there behind that dark door

Is a path, which leads through the brain.

No one knows, no one dares to go

And look behind the door

And follow the path

And follow the path.

To seek in the mystic depths

And find – ?

Alison M. Graham

Chapter One
The Lecture

In that strange luminous light of a stormy autumn day the wind was gusting across the park trying to pluck the trees from their lakeside homes and dash them into the lake, trying to rip the water from the lake and deposit it where the trees stood but just stopped short of doing both. Instead it threw itself with a wild intensity against the windows of our small lecture theatre on the second floor of the Western Bank building, plastering them momentarily with spray and then just as quickly wiping them clean again. It was the sort of autumn afternoon to be looking out of a window and watching the antics of the wind and rain. It was not one to be joining in those antics, to find oneself alternately flung across the path or plastered with wet, soggy, brown, decaying leaves – leaves which had been finally persuaded to leave their summer homes for the joy of a brief, wild helter-skelter on the vortices of the wind before being finally betrayed and dumped unceremoniously in some gutter or hedgerow, there to await the road sweeper's broom.

It was the sort of autumn afternoon to be standing with one's back to a roaring log fire or sitting comfortably curled up in a big armchair with a good book. As it happened, I was doing neither of these things. This particular afternoon I was sitting in a small lecture theatre listening, or supposed to be listening, to Professor Stewart giving a lecture in his series on "The Growth and Development of Industry". Tonight I would have to write an essay on the afternoon's subject, and tomorrow we would have a tutorial in which each of us in turn would have to discuss our essays. This approach normally made me particularly attentive, in order to glean as much subject material as possible. However, this particular afternoon the professor's voice was merely a pleasant drone in the background. That morning I had been particularly busy with my final year thesis. I had in fact spent it in the old library down in the Engineering Building at St George's Square. I preferred to work in the old library rather than the new one on Western Bank. It was more comfortable. Its small friendly bays between the rows of mature bookshelves imparted a womb-like comfort, ideal for studying. Just an hour earlier I had remembered this lecture, had finished off my work in the library, and braced myself for the walk through the churchyard, up the hill against the wind and rain. Somehow, on the way, the beauty of the autumn afternoon and the strange light had impinged onto my technical brain and I'd arrived at Western Bank in a strange frame of mind. I was more tuned to the weather than I was to Professor Stewart.

This series of lectures was about the Humane Aspects of Industry, such subjects as dust control, atmospheric pollution, respiratory, diseases related to industry, and so on. Professor Stewart was a recognised expert in this field, a dedicated man, whose enthusiasm for his subject was contagious, and he always managed to fill his small lecture theatre, even though the subject was not a compulsory one for the course. The subject this afternoon was "The economics of a Control Room". It was of particular interest to me as I intended embarking on a career in instrument and control engineering when I left university, and I had looked forward to this lecture for some time. Yet there I was, despite all my previous interest, taking no notice whatsoever. I was hypnotised by the warmth of the theatre, the wind lashing at the windows, and the strange eerie light of that wild afternoon. I was pleasantly relaxed and my mind almost not working at all when I suddenly became aware that I was no longer watching the weather but must have been examining the medical specimens around the room. *I was suddenly very aware of studying intently a brain.*

This brain was a very old one and was in fact bottled in some sort of preservative. Professor Stewart decorated the sides of his lecture theatre with specimens which had had some particular interest to him in his work. Presumably, this brain had had something wrong with it of particular note which had caused him to keep it. It wasn't what was wrong with it, however, that held my interest. In fact, I never really knew what *had* attracted my interest, but that mouldy old brain was certainly to give me nightmares, and I was to wish many times in the years ahead that I had stayed in St George's Library that autumn day. That was, however, as yet, in the future.

As I was saying, my attention was riveted on this old brain, and suddenly my own was working again, not on the lecture subject but on what was a new strange track. It was asking itself some questions Why is the human brain as large as that? Why do we only use one-third of it? Why can't we use the other two-thirds? The human body normally adapts itself over many years to eliminate what it doesn't use, or grows to accommodate the most used organs. So what is the other two-thirds of the brain for? Was it used much more extensively in the past, or is it growing to an appropriate size for some future use?

The professor's voice had faded even further into the background now and the wind no longer impinged on my consciousness. It must have had something to do with the strange light, but I seemed to be in tune with that old brain. It was impossible for it to have a latent power of course, but somehow, from somewhere, I felt a sense of throbbing power bubbling in the atmosphere around me, but I couldn't make use of it. There was an energy source close – so close – but I just couldn't reach it.

The brain weighs three and a half pounds and it contains ten billion nerve cells. The power of that organic computer was potentially unlimited but remained virtually untapped.

"Tim, are you okay?" Suddenly the outside world fought its way into my mind by virtue of Professor Stewart shaking my shoulder with some concern. The lecture was obviously over, leaving one or two of my friends and the professor who seemed to think I'd been in a coma or ill or something. I shook my head. I was bathed in sweat.

"Yes, I think I'm okay."

"What happened, Tim?" Frank Cooper, my oldest friend at the university, asked anxiously.

I was suddenly looking at that old bottled brain again, but this time it had no effect. The hammering I heard this time was the wind redoubling its efforts against the window.

"Frank," I asked, "do you know what the greatest wonder of the world is and the greatest unsolved mystery?"

"Are you *sure* that you are okay?" he persisted.

I ignored his question.

"It's something we carry around with us all the time and take it for granted," I continued. "It's the human brain."

Chapter Two
An Experience at Fountains Abbey

Isn't it strange that you can experience sensations and feelings as strong as I did that afternoon in the Western Bank building in Sheffield and yet, within a very short time, forget all about them. That is exactly what happened to me in 1962. My brain, perhaps worried at the experience, sorted it and filed it in some far-away dusty corner, and my conscious mind carried on with its main function which was to obtain the best possible degree it was capable of. It spent the rest of that year and half of the following year parrying all demands made on it from the outside world, and was on the whole pretty successful, for I graduated that summer with a First Class Honours Degree in Electrical Engineering. It was as unexpected as it was welcome. My brain had surprised me, whatever and wherever the *me* bit was.

Anyway, as I was saying, whatever else my brain had beaten off or filed away in my subconscious during that last traumatic year at university, it made a pretty good job of forgetting that particular autumn afternoon, when I had felt for some seconds that I was on the verge of some world-shattering revelation. It drew a veil so completely and utterly that I never gave it a thought for another sixteen years – sixteen years in which I made good use of my education, widening and expanding it all the time. I completed a graduate apprenticeship with British Railways in York and went on to design signalling and telecommunication systems during the period when British Railways was modernising its signalling network. I followed that up with a couple of years helping to design and commission complex control systems in nuclear power stations, in particular at the Wylfa Power Station on Anglesey in North Wales. In all this time I had moved around Britain and stayed in some beautiful places full of history and emotion. I'd walked the walls of York City regularly during my four years in York. I'd imagined myself a Roman soldier looking from the city across the northern plains towards the far-away Hadrian's Wall. I'd stood on that very wall myself, at Housesteads Fort, on the crest of Whin Sill on a misty evening just as the sun was setting blood red into the distant horizon. I'd experienced the mysticism of the Holy Isle off the Northumbrian coast on a warm but misty afternoon and many other places, but none of them had ever even partially re-created for me the feelings of immensity of power and of loneliness that I'd experienced that afternoon in Western Bank. They hadn't even triggered the remembrance. The correct bells hadn't been rung, the hooks were always missing. Missing that is until I visited Fountains Abbey, near Ripon, in North Yorkshire.

By 1969 1 had moved back to the area where I'd been born. To Teesside. But then, I had been born and raised in Grangetown so I knew pretty well what Teesside was all about, and although I went to work for a firm on the South Bank of the Tees, engaged in the contracting industry, I had decided to live out of reach of the mists, smoke, fumes, and noises of the industry, and so I rented a bungalow just outside the industrial conurbation. Some years later I moved firms again, this time to work on the North Bank of the Tees. At the same time I decided to move further away from the town and set about searching for a country cottage. It was several years before I found what I was looking for, in a tiny North Yorkshire village that I'd never previously heard of.

I finally moved in during the late summer of 1979 and settled in very quickly. At weekends it became my custom to investigate some part of the countryside around. My new cottage gave me a base in an area I'd not previously explored. One Saturday in October I set out to visit Fountains Abbey. Fountains Abbey, I had been told, was considered to be among the outstanding monastic ruins of Western Europe. I set out before lunch and drove over to Ripon where I discovered a very nice place serving lunches. Consequently it was getting on for three o'clock before I approached Fountains through Studley Royal Park. I didn't see any of the famous deer as I drove through the park, but I did notice that there was a stiff breeze getting up. By the time I'd parked the car near to the lake and walked along to buy my entrance ticket I was beginning to doubt whether I should bother at all, because there were some rather menacing looking clouds starting to obscure the rather pleasant autumn sunshine. My indecision carried me through the gates, and the Custodian for the Department of the Environment settled the issue by handing me a ticket and demanding money in exchange. I paid automatically and followed the path up the side of the River Skell as it wound its way through the woods towards the Abbey. It was quite sheltered on the path, but high above me the trees were swaying and the wind created a continuous sound of roaring in the branches as the breeze steadily turned into a strong wind.

In twenty minutes I was in sight of the Abbey with its huge tower. The pathway passes along above the Abbey which is built in the valley, and I walked along its length and then turned and descended from the path across the well-cut green towards the nave entrance where I passed into the ruins of that once great church.

It was empty; all the other visitors had given best to the wind and threatening rain. Only I stood in that historic ruin with the wind growing more violent by the second as, after its long chase across the open parkland, it was suddenly funnelled through the door of the building to expand into the ruins and roar out through the roof, open to the skies, suddenly and joyfully freed again from artificial constraints. It came in through the empty windows and spaces of missing masonry, it tumbled and swirled and carried with it the debris of an autumn day. Brown leaves and dust, waste paper and cigarette ends, and perhaps also music and laughter or light and darkness. As I walked up the ancient aisle towards the raised altar, the wind seemed to change the light, and the stark pointing wall piers, which had once held a rose window behind the high altar, formed a frame around a strangely purple, reddish sky producing an eerie effect. Then as I mounted the altar steps with ruined pillars all around me holding up that strangely lit sky, the wind, as if on command, perhaps an ancient command, dropped away. All around, it surged and battered, but there in the centre of the church I was becalmed in the eye of the turbulence within the stone walls.

The magic of that moment provided the secret codes to unlock the memory of that day in the Western Bank building in Sheffield seventeen years before, and with a sense of shock the memory of that experience flooded out from its secret prison in my mind. As the locks gave way and the imprisoning doors swung open, I remembered that old brain and my thought of that moment. It came back to me very strongly – the greatest wonder of the world and the greatest mystery – the recollection of this thought pulsing its way into my conscious mind acted like a bridge, a bridge from my awareness of the physical world around me to. . . to something. What that something was I had no idea, and later I had extreme difficulty in describing that second. The Abbey Church around me faded. It didn't disappear. I was still faintly aware of the stark ruin, but it had lost its hard physical reality and I was suddenly aware of a power. Where that power came from I couldn't decide. It was unfocused, it came in waves at random intervals with no apparent linking between. Sometimes the energy tumbled and crashed around me, and at other times it was just a gentle murmur. But I was conscious of a great powerhouse of stored, yet fully mobile, energy. I tried to concentrate on it, but I was newly aware and still in shock and had no control whatsoever over the phenomenon. Momentarily, during one of the more gentle murmurs of pouring energy, I detected something else, almost as though I was aware of someone standing beside me. Someone as puzzled as I was. Yes, certainly puzzled, perhaps even a little afraid. Before I could stop myself I reached out to reassure, but suddenly it was gone. I was alone in the rapidly darkening ruins. The feeling that someone was with me had been so strong that I turned quickly, sure that someone was there. But no, empty walls and pillars were all that kept me company that evening. Then the rain came in through the open roof to join us and to bring me back to the real world around me, and I decided that it was time to head for my car.

As I wound my way back to the car park, partially shielded from the pelting rain by the protective arch of trees above, I tried to reconstruct the experience again, but it was fading rapidly and what I had seen so clearly a few minutes earlier was becoming as muddy as the water running on the path beneath my feet. I reached the gate to find an impatient custodian waiting to lock the gate behind me.

"Sorry to keep you!"

"That's okay, sir," Polite with it, he was too.

"In fact you are only just the last out, sir. The young lady came out only a few minutes ago."

The gate slammed behind us and the tumblers of the big old lock fell into place.

"What young lady? *I* didn't see anyone else there at all."

The keeper gave me an odd sideways look as he stopped at his car and pointed to another car just leaving the car park.

"I'm surprised you didn't see her, sir. She arrived at about the same time as you did, although it could have been a few minutes after you. Goodnight, sir." He slammed his car door shut, which precluded any further questions, and anyway, I was getting wet out in the open so I made my way quickly to the car.

I struggled out of my wet coat and turned on the engine. The windscreen had quickly fogged up with condensation and I turned on the blower to clear the windscreen, together with the back window heater, and sat for a few minutes waiting for them to clear. I still hadn't really come round from my 'experience' and it took quite an effort to shake my mind into a state to drive and to follow the gatekeeper's car down the road through the Studley Royal Park back towards Ripon. For some reason I had a strong mental impression of the other car as well – a white Ford Escort as it was driven away by a young lady.

A sudden thought struck me and I turned on the inside light to look at my watch. Seven thirty-eight! I'd gone into the park at about four o'clock. Twenty minutes to walk to the church and twenty back again, ten minutes since I came out of the gates. That made a grand total of 50 minutes. That meant that I'd been in the church for just over two and a half hours somehow. Yet I'd have sworn that it was only about ten minutes or so. No wonder the gatekeeper had looked at me oddly. What about the unknown young lady? Had I met her and not been able to remember? Had she come across me in a trance? If so, why hadn't she gone for help? As I drove into Ripon market place I remembered the feeling of someone near me. It didn't make sense, something was not right. I laughed at myself then with that thought and decided to have a pint of beer and forget about it.

This time, however, I didn't forget it. Two pints and an evening meal later I sat down at home with a bedtime coffee and my usual accompanying noise from the stereo and mused over what had happened. I just could not get over losing time like that. What had happened? Why had it happened, and perhaps more importantly, would it happen again? Consideration of that particular question sent me along another track. It was the second time it had happened, and each time something had triggered it – but what? I fell asleep that night, being no further forward. I was sure that it was nothing so superficial as the weather, even though the two days *had* been fairly similar, but I must have seen dozens of such days in my life without the same effect. No, it wasn't that, there was something else, another key.

I eventually dozed off with little or no progress made, much to my annoyance, and then when I awoke I had the answer – or had I?

I hadn't been awakened by the usual dulcet tones of the radio alarm clock. It was there yes, peering at me with its soft green electronic light, but it was still early – 4.10 a.m. It radiated through the darkness as I peered at it. Now, usually I don't wake during the night and I had a distinct feeling of being awakened. What had it been? I listened intently for a noise, but no, there was nothing. I wasn't cold. My thoughts drifted, trying to penetrate the darkness. Thoughts produced by my sleepy brain. I sat up in bed. *Brain* – that was it, the link; each time I had thought of the Prof.'s old preserved brain bottled up in a preservative. My sleeping brain had unlocked the mystery, or had it? Perhaps it had put two of the keys together and unlocked another chain of thought leading to another mystery – the greatest mystery of the world – the brain. Now that was the key, but this time nothing happened. I could feel the phrase ringing in my ears. I could remember it very clearly from that day, now long gone, in Sheffield, and again yesterday, that was the phrase that had set whatever happened into motion, but tonight – not a thing. I could hear the rustling of the trees outside but gently now as the storm subsided.

I was disturbed for the remainder of the night, really only dozing fitfully, and I was ready to get up when the alarm eventually did go off. Almost fearfully, I remembered what I'd thought during the night. At least it hadn't been a dream which disappeared, as those profound night thoughts are wont to do.

I drove to work thoughtfully that morning. I never really noticed the minor roads across to the A19 but took my usual care going up the very narrow lane up Cotcliffe Bank, but it was all automatic, and before I realised it I was speeding along over the new Tees bridge in the middle lane.

I parked my car at work in my usual spot and took the stairs to the second floor, where my office was located in the furthest corner of the building, hiding me away from all but the most determined visitors. I picked up a cup of coffee from the machine en route and headed along the corridor nodding and muttering the usual good mornings.

"Morning, Tim." My reverie was finally broken by Bob Atwell.

Bob lived in the next office to mine and was a mechanical engineer. We often had work in common and usually lunched together because we tended to think about things and people in a similar way.

"You were miles away then. Are you having trouble with that computer again?"

"Sorry, Bob. Good morning. No, it's got nothing to do with that thing." We were in the final stages of acceptance trials for a dual computer system for our latest chemical plant, but we were having some real problems with it.

"To tell you the truth, Bob, I'd forgotten all about that computer." I walked into his office with him.

"In fact, you just might be interested in this little problem. It's just up your street." Bob was an avid science fiction fan.

I turned to his notice-board and absent-mindedly flicked over his calendar from September to October.

"I wish you'd keep yourself up to date."

"I always leave that for you to do," he laughed, taking out his handkerchief and cleaning his rimless glasses ready for the day's work.

"What were you going to tell me? – don't get side tracked."

"Have you ever been to Sheffield?"

"Yes, once, on a course last year, to the university. I was—"

"And have you been to Fountains Abbey?" I rudely interrupted him. He ignored the rudeness as we were good enough friends to be rude to each other most of the time.

"Yes, I have." He paused, waiting for the next question while he took his jacket off and put it in his locker.

I walked across to the window and put my coffee down on the window ledge. I gazed out over the acid tanks, pipe bridges, and warehouses which bordered the river, over the cranes and city rooftops to the swell of the Eston Hills, their summit crowned by "The Nab" and a tropospheric scatter aerial for Phillips Petroleum offshore installations.

"Well. . ." I turned to find him sitting at his desk, hands behind his head, leaning back in his chair, face all expectant, waiting for me to go on. ". . .I was at Fountains yesterday and. . ." and I told him all about the strange experience and also about my earlier one years ago in Sheffield.

I finished, swigged my coffee down, and threw the polystyrene cup into the filing tray in the corner, usually called a waste bin.

"What do you think?"

He hadn't said a word. In fact he hadn't moved. Suddenly he let the chair fall back onto its four legs and banged his two hands onto his desk.

"Hey! You are dead serious, aren't you?"

"Yes, of course."

"Sorry, Tim, at first I thought you were kidding, but about half way through I realised you were serious. You *have* got problems, haven't you?"

He was like that – straight and direct, as you might expect someone from the West Riding of Yorkshire to be.

"It's very interesting that, you know." He'd taken me at my word. He didn't disbelieve me and there he was, as interested as me, and suddenly he was throwing ideas out. That was Bob's technique. He used people as sounding boards and most of his ideas fell to the floor immediately, but some of them resonated and were taken up with varying degrees of success. We weren't having too much joy this morning, though, and we both fell silent for a few minutes. I was about to head for my own office to start work when he threw his pencil on the desk.

"Do you get the *Gazette*?" He pushed his glasses with a forefinger.

"Yes, why?"

"If you looked at last Wednesday's edition, there was an article on the brain."

"No, I didn't see that one. Last Wednesday. . . I would have been out at a Parish Council meeting."

"I'll bring it in tomorrow." He was chuckling to himself.

"Well, what did it say?"

"No, I'll bring it in tomorrow. I don't want to guess at what it said. If the wife hasn't used it to peel potatoes into, I'll bring it in."

I knew Bob of old and could tell that he wasn't going any further this morning, and so I left him to it with an appropriate remark about secretive people. All he did was laugh in my face. But, true to his word, same time same place next morning, before he took his coat off he opened his briefcase and pulled out a newspaper and flung it across the desk towards me.

"There you are. I managed to save it in the nick of time from the dustbin."

It certainly looked as though it had come from the waste bin, and at the very least it had had potato peelings in. I smoothed out the newspaper cutting and laid it on his desk.

Bob was grinning to himself as he poked his hat into his locker and stripped off to his waistcoat. The very first sentence of the article had hit me straight between the eyes:

> The Greatest wonder of the world and the greatest unsolved mystery is something we all carry around with us and take for granted – The Human Brain

"Didn't *you* say something like that yesterday?" Bob slammed the locker door shut and leaned against the window ledge.

I had to admit to having just that sentiment as I quickly scanned the very brief article which was a review of a new book. It didn't take one any further than the basic statement, which was a shade disappointing.

"What was so good about it that you had to keep it secret yesterday?" Bob leaned across to the desk and whistled the slip of paper into his hand.

"You still haven't seen it, have you?" he chuckled.

"Look at the author of the book." He thrust the paper back under my nose.

"What did you say your professor at Sheffield was called – wasn't it Stewart? Look! Who's written this book? J. N. Stewart. If you are really serious about this thing, *that*, my friend, is an omen from the gods and therefore a starting point not to be missed." He tried to stuff his hands into his waistcoat pockets and wandered up and down his office quite excited. It was infectious and solidified the idea in my own mind that had been swirling around for the last few days.

"Yes," I said, absent-mindedly drumming on the window ledge with my knuckles and looking out into the Teesside mists.

"Yes, that's it. You have it, Bob. I have to go with this thing. I'll give him a ring and see if I can meet him again to have a chat about it."

"Don't forget," he shouted at me as I left his office, "any help you want, just give me a call. It sounds as though this could be right interesting. It'll make a change anyway from pipes and blowers. In fact," he shouted at me as I departed down the corridor, "I'll be most upset if you don't keep me up-to-date."

Chapter Three
The Temple of Mithras

It was the end of the week before I had finally established the whereabouts of Professor Stewart. He was in the USA for another two weeks.

"It's most frustrating, you know," I muttered to Bob as we walked along the road going to lunch on Friday.

"There I am all worked up and he won't be back for another fortnight."

"Well, apart from a quick trip to the States, which I don't think that you can justify, you'll just have to work yourself down again. What are you doing this weekend?"

A quick change of subject was another of Bob's quirks and it required an agile mind to keep up with him sometimes.

"Oh, nothing much. I'm supposed to be visiting a friend with whom I was at university. He lives in Newcastle now. He's married, but it does have its advantages."

"You mean being married?"

"No, I mean *him* being married. It means that I get a good slap-up meal this Sunday, which I wouldn't normally get."

The friend I was visiting was Frank Cooper. He'd been married six years after we left college and he now had a little girl of four years old called Gillian.

"Actually, now I think about it. . ." – we raced across the road in front of a petrol tanker which was intent on mowing us down and smothering us in its foul, furry breath – ". . .the very same man was present in Western Bank during—"

"I'm supposed to have changed the subject away from that subject, you know. It's not allowed again today."

"Okay, okay, sorry – what's Middlesborough going to do this weekend?" Football was a safe subject, guaranteed to start a good argument at the lunch table.

Bob might have changed the subject, but I couldn't do it that well, though I tried. I tried right through the Saturday, and managed not to bring it up at all when I went to Frank Cooper's for Sunday lunch. I arrived as usual at about twelve noon just in time to go through the conventional farce of dragging Frank away from his wife, Eileen, to visit the pub for a quick pint of beer at the local. We met so rarely these days that I found it very pleasant to sit with a pint and go over old times and talk about what had happened to so and so and. . . That particular Sunday, however, though I tried hard, I was obviously not keeping up my end of the conversation very well because Frank suddenly asked if I felt okay.

"Yes, why?" I was taken aback a little.

"Well, I've been telling you all about meeting Ian in London last week and unless I'm mistaken you've not taken in a word. All you've done is to stare through your glass of beer."

"Sorry, Frank. I must truly admit to not listening to you." I looked at the clock.

"I'll tell you about it later, but look at the time. It's time we were getting back for lunch or your Eileen will be at us."

He nodded and finished off his drink. "Okay, later then."

I enjoyed the expected formal Sunday lunch complete with a nice bottle of white wine, and with all the general chatter I did gradually relax and almost forgot about my preoccupation.

It was one of those pleasant warm sunny October afternoons that we sometimes get. A complete change from the weekend previously.

Eileen wanted to go out for a drive, and we debated where we should go while we ploughed through the washing up.

"What about Housesteads?" It was Frank's suggestion. It sent a tingle through me which started at the base of my spine and slowly and laboriously worked its way up my backbone to dissipate itself finally in my neck, causing a general shiver.

Eileen noticed. "Are you cold?"

"No, I'm not." I looked oddly at Frank.

"It was your mention of Housesteads." I hadn't yet told him of my strange experience at Fountains and I think he was beginning to think that I really was odd.

"What has Housesteads to do with your shivering?"

"I'm not really sure, but—" at that point little Gillian started screaming her head off and everyone, including me, forgot about my explanation. Gillian had managed to get her hand stuck in a toy and she had decided that she needed attention. From that flurry of activity we progressed to getting ready to go out, and off we went in Frank's car heading for the Wall.

In the far north of England everyone, of course, knows what the Wall is. The Wall – Hadrian's Wall – was built on the instructions of the Roman Emperor Hadrian during a visit to Britain in – well, sometime in the second century AD. My feeling for history doesn't extend to exact dates.

Today, almost two thousand years later, much of the Wall can still be seen, snaking its way through the border country. It is still possible to walk along much of its length, and Frank had in fact walked its length from Wallsend to the Solway Coast.

This Sunday, however, he assured us that we were out only for a short walk to visit Housesteads Fort. Housesteads was one of the best-known forts on the wall and it covered several acres of land.

We parked the car in the car park just off the main road and started on the field path to the fort. Gillian had decided that it was Uncle Tim's day and refused to leave me, but decided that she didn't want to walk at all. A piggyback was the only solution, and really it was just as well because the ground was quite muddy and uneven. In fact, halfway there we were beginning to think that it hadn't been such a good idea after all. By the time we struggled up the hill to the fort the sun was settling towards the horizon. The muddy walk had been well worthwhile. Standing on the Wall at Housesteads at sunset was always a fantastic, emotional experience – particularly on this Sunday. It was a fine example of the season of mists and mellow fruitfulness. The mist was just sufficient to produce a haze around the setting sun as it changed its golden cloak for its red evening wear. It was not sufficient to hide the majestic, awe-inspiring view of the Wall as it soared in great majesty over the Whin Sill. For nearly two thousand years it had been standing, the eternal guardian, looking to the north, guarding against the seeming vast expanses of hills and forests and moorland. Today with the mists curling around its base and softening the military harshness, even Gillian could sense the feeling of awe, the feeling, perhaps not of eternity, but something close to it.

As the sun dropped lower, and longer shadows were being cast, Eileen broke the spell with a shiver.

"Frank, it's time we were getting back. It's getting quite chilly and I don't want Gillian getting cold."

"Right, come on then." I gathered my human shadow up and swung Gillian up onto my shoulders.

"Come on, Gilly, let's race Daddy back to the car."

The last of the Roman mysteries seemed to have been dispelled as we galloped down the slope amidst shouting and laughter. As we left the immediate area of the Wall, I was regretting the challenge to race because the going was still muddy and it was quite an effort with little Gillian on my shoulders.

Trying not to get too far in front of us, Frank and Eileen had negotiated the field quite well and were heading for the gate towards the car park as we, or rather I, gathered my last resource of energy and, aided by the slight slope, started running again with Gillian shrieking with excitement.

Suddenly the shrieks of laughter turned to shrieks of fear. I lost my footing and, slipping and sliding down the slope, I tried to balance Gillian on my shoulders as I fell rather acrobatically into the grass. I managed to twist from under her as I fell and so she wasn't damaged by my weight at all, but we both hit the ground with a fairly hefty thump. Paradoxically, the mud now helped. Had the ground been hard, we would have been hurt quite badly. As it was, the mud cushioned Gillian's fall, and she was little the worse for the incident apart from being extremely muddy. My initial fall too was cushioned, but I skidded further down the slope and over a small vertical drop and knocked my head on a stone.

The world about me dimmed and Gillian's shrieking receded into the distance. It didn't quite disappear, but it receded behind the thick stone walls which I perceived were about me. For a moment, time stood still as I listened to the old priest intoning his litany to the Persian sun god. I tried to lean against the wooden pillar in the temple as my senses swam. I had to clutch something for support and as I put out my bands to the pillar my foot caught in the hem of my toga and I fell. As I fell, my head thumped against the altar stone and I passed out momentarily.

As I struggled back to consciousness my head was throbbing and the full volume of Gillian screaming was searing its way into the centre of the throb. I was helped to a sitting position in the damp grass by an anxious-looking Frank. As I wiped the blood from my eyes and discovered that I wasn't seriously maimed, the level of screaming reduced and the impact on my senses was one of relief.

"Gillian?"

"She's okay, Tim, just shaken up and frightened; but how about you?"

"I think I'm okay." I looked around me at the darkening landscape. I had an uninterrupted view of the fields except for the two-foot bank that I rolled over and bashed my head on – the only protruding stone to be seen in this area.

"You've been pretty unlucky to hit your head on that," Frank commented, mistaking my look as if I was looking for what I'd banged my head on – but I was looking for the very solid walls that I'd been surrounded by a moment ago.

"Come on, let's get you back to the car. I don't think you've broken anything, but you're not doing your suit any good sitting in that mud." With a great deal of help I managed to get to my feet and was helped back to the car into which I collapsed gratefully. Gillian was having nothing to do with me. She'd stopped crying now, but was cuddling in to her mum. Uncle Tim was out of favour. He did nasty things like throwing her to the ground.

We were both in a pretty muddy state. Arriving back at Frank's, Eileen ran me a hot bath and I had a good scrape before sitting down in front of the fire in some borrowed clothes.

As the flames leapt eagerly up the chimney, steadily working their way through the black coal, turning it into red heat and, having consumed it, dropping it without a thought through the grate, my mind was in a turmoil. I still had a headache, despite the aspirins, but I was thinking quite clearly.

"Frank, have you got an Ordnance Survey map of the Wall?"

He was on one of his excursions from the kitchen, where he was helping to prepare tea, into the restfully lit lounge to make sure that I was still in one piece.

"Sure, yes, there should be one in here somewhere." He peered at the bookcase and after several false starts produced the required map.

"Here you are. What's your problem?"

I spread the map out and tried to find the Housesteads area.

"I've just had an idea."

"If you'd tell me, perhaps I could help."

"Where's Housesteads on here for a start?"

We both knelt on the carpet peering at the map.

"There it is – look." Frank's questing forefinger had found it first. Mine took over and traced the path back from the fort towards the road until I'd roughly located the spot where I'd fallen. There was nothing shown, just one of those brown contour lines wiggling its way around.

"Mmm." I obviously sounded pensive.

Frank was starting to get impatient, though he was trying to hide it.

"What were you looking for?"

I answered his question with another one which, in retrospect, I'm sure he found most annoying.

"Do you have a guide book of the Wall?"

"Yes, I think so." He made no voluntary effort to look for it, so I pushed him.

"Do you think I could see it?"

"Yes, if you tell me what you are looking for."

"Get the book first and be patient, Frank. Humour an injured man." I put my hand up to my plastered forehead.

"Okay, okay. There it is." He found it in the bookcase and threw it across to me and departed off in a semi huff to continue with his tea preparations.

Actually, it was Eileen who was preparing tea, and after Frank had put several things in the wrong dishes he was kicked out of the kitchen and had to return to me.

"What have you found?"

I had the guide open at a page which had an old map of the Wall, made in the nineteenth century. It clearly showed Housesteads, but also it had a bit more detail on than the Ordnance Survey map.

"There, look at that."

Frank squinted at the page and the point that my finger was indicating.

"Mithraic Temple (site)," he read out loud and leaned back with a puzzled expression as though he thought that the knock on the head had indeed done me some damage.

"So?" He waited for an explanation.

"Don't you see? That is exactly the place where I fell over this afternoon."

"So?" He repeated his question.

I could see the expressions on his face as I outlined my experience on the field. The dim lighting in the room and the leaping firelight imparted a chisel-like quality to the features and seemed to etch them clearly, showing his thoughts. Now he really did think that I'd suffered some damage.

"But, Tim, you only fell over and I turned back to you immediately. You weren't even unconscious."

"Nevertheless, I was in that Mithraic Temple." I pointed at the old map.

"I think we'd better have some tea." Eileen had appeared silently and had obviously also heard the conversation because she too was looking at me rather oddly.

It was by now well past a normal Sunday teatime. Gillian had been put to bed. and so it was a relatively calm atmosphere instead of the hurly-burly of lunch.

I decided that I would have to prove that I was still sane, and so I asked Frank to think back over the years to our Sheffield days.

"Frank, do you remember Professor Stewart?"

He stopped cutting up the very appetising looking pizza. He had a startled look.

"My God." He waved the knife at me. "That day in the lecture theatre on Western Bank."

I nodded, a little taken aback at his immediate recollection of the incident.

"Do you know what happened?"

Frank nodded thoughtfully and commenced working on the pizza again. A large piece had been excavated for each of us and was on our individual plates before he spoke again. He put the handle of the knife on the table with the blade pointing at the ceiling.

"You passed out, and when you came to you said. . ." – he tapped the table slowly with the knife handle – ". . .and I quote, 'Frank, do you know what the greatest wonder of the world is and the greatest unsolved mystery?'"

That little cool shiver chased itself across my back again.

"Yes," I answered in a whisper, "that's exactly what I did say."

"Surely you're not connecting the two incidents?"

"I must admit that until this moment I wasn't doing so, other than in a superficial way, but yes, now you've remembered that, I *do* connect them, but not only because of these two apparently unrelated incidents. There has been another. . ."

I then went on to tell them about my experience at Fountains Abbey the previous weekend.

When I'd finished, there was silence for several minutes with only the crackling from the fire and the burbling from the coffee percolator intruding.

Frank shook his head, his broad forehead creased with a frown.

"But, Tim, it's too incredible. You have to be making it up."

"Why? Why does he have to be making it up?" I suddenly seemed to have an ally in Eileen. "You, you're so logical that you can't take anything on trust." I must admit that I was a little startled at her outburst. She was obviously repeating a favourite criticism of Frank. "You can't reject it just like that. If Tim says it happened like that, it *did*."

I looked at her, suspicious that she was humouring me, but no, she was deadly serious. I nodded as Frank turned back to me.

"Yes," I agreed with him, "it *is* unbelievable and. . ." – I included Eileen – ". . .*not* logical, but nevertheless something has happened, or is definitely happening, to me. Perhaps I really have had a bad knock and I am going round the bend."

"Okay, okay." Frank always said okay twice. He couldn't use it on its own.

"Suppose we accept, for the moment. . ." – he was grudging about acceptance – ". . .that what you say has happened is true. No. . ." – he rethought his words again – ". . .not quite that. Suppose we accept that what you *think* happened really did happen." Frank was happier with the revised version.

"I tell you it did. . ."

"Okay, okay." He held his hand up to stop me. "Let me go on. Have you thought what the implications are? You are talking about the transmission of yourself through time. . . momentarily. *If* you really were in a Mithraic Temple this afternoon."

It was Frank's cool logical computer training. He set off on a course, as a programmer. To get from A to B there had to be a programmed course. A jump from one program to another unrelated was forbidden.

I looked into his steel grey eyes for some moments.

"You read too many science fiction books, Frank. There has got to be a simpler explanation than that."

"Simpler? How can you find a simpler explanation, Tim?" Eileen was worried and was starting to collect the pots together.

I shook my head. "Most things are simple when explained: it's the explanation that's difficult. Do you realise that for the greater part of the time our minds work along predefined patterns. Patterns of thought that we've used time and time again. We get into a rut and when we do get an idea, and I mean a really *new* idea, we are really pleased with ourselves. The achievement of jumping out of the pattern is really stimulating." We'd moved to sit in front of the fire again and Frank plumped down onto the settee.

"I must admit," he mused almost to himself, "that you do sound sane, but there *has* to be a reason."

"Exactly, there has to be a reason, but what is it? Normal logical thought isn't going to solve it. Lateral thinking is what we need."

Frank laughed relieving the serious tone of the conversation.

"You just sounded like one of those lecturers on a management course."

"Sorry, but it's true."

"So, where has your lateral thinking got you?"

"Nowhere yet, I must admit, except that I've made an appointment to see Professor Stewart a week tomorrow." Frank suddenly sat up with interest.

"Have you now? That's interesting. . . And that was before this afternoon?"

"Yes," I agreed, "this afternoon has only served to reinforce my feeling that I need some new thinking on the problem."

"You've got just the right man there to give you that," Frank agreed and he went on to explain to Eileen who and what Professor Stewart was.

"You mean, he's a doctor?"

"Well, no. Although he was a medical doctor, I think, he is also a qualified PhD, which means that he's called Doctor, anyway." Frank was appealing for help in explaining what Stewart was exactly, but in all honesty I couldn't really define it exactly either.

"He's. . . well, the simplest explanation is to say, I suppose, that he is something of a neurologist but with a further interest in problems that arise in industry due to environment, etc.."

Eileen nodded. "You mean, he's an expert on the nervous system?"

"Yes, something like that."

"Have you got a nervous problem then?" She was still puzzled. I took a deep breath, feeling myself getting deeper and deeper into the water.

"No, or rather, I don't think so. I wouldn't want to exclude it altogether. But, you see, all this started at Professor Stewart's lecture." Frank had jumped in so fast earlier on that it hadn't been explained to Eileen just what had happened at the lecture. I went through it all again for her benefit with Frank nodding and mm..ing in the right places to confirm the points.

"And so you see," I concluded, "that old brain all pasty white, with all its knots and whorls, swimming in an old bottle full of ageing yellow preservative, is one of the keys to this matter, and if it is in Professor Stewart's lecture room, he must have had something to do with it."

"And so you are going to see Professor Stewart." Eileen nodded. Even Frank was appreciative of the logic here.

The talk went on and on and around the subject, but didn't advance the theory any further, and finally I had to call a halt.

"Look at the time. It's a quarter to ten. By the time I get back it will be a quarter past eleven and I've got to go into work early tomorrow." Eileen took the hint and jumped up.

"A cup of coffee before you go, then you can go straight to bed when you get home."

So I was pressurised into another drink and some supper, and it was half past ten when I finally edged my way to the door.

"Oh, Frank, I nearly forgot – do you think I could borrow that guide for a while?"

"Yes, no problem," he replied, picking it up and passing it to me.

I left Newcastle with another two people interested in my problem. Perhaps even more so than Bob Atwell – after all, they had actually been present when I'd had my latest 'thing'.

'Thing' was so inadequate a way to describe what had happened, yet I didn't know a better one. Not yet, anyway.

I threaded my way through the tunnels and crossovers that made up the A1(M) through Newcastle centre and finally got out onto the A1 to the South. It was a quiet clear night with little traffic on the road, and for the first time since the afternoon I was on my own. On my own to think about that moment in time when I felt myself to be a Roman soldier.

A Roman soldier in the Temple of Mithras at Housesteads Fort on the frontier of the Roman Empire.

Chapter Four
Meeting with the Professor

I first went to Sheffield when I went for an interview at the Engineering Department of the university in 1960. I always remember that day. I was terrified. It was my first interview for a university place and the word itself at that time had an aura of grandness and learning which made me feel terribly small and insignificant. The day didn't help. It was one of those bleak Yorkshire days with a heavy drizzle helping to damp the slightest sign of any joy. One of the rapidly dying breed of steam engines puffed into the dour and blackened Midland Station and deposited me in that forbidding strange city. I took one look at the place, and my stomach dropped even further into my boots. The city was in the process of being raised like a phoenix from is own ashes. There were still many signs of the wartime blitz around, with boarded-up buildings and waste sites, and the whole place looked unbearably dreary. As I rode through the centre on the Number 95 bus I resolved there and then that Sheffield was not the place for me whatever happened at my interview.

Dr Harrison unknowingly changed all that at the interview. He was a kind, gentle, white-haired man. No doubt he had interviewed many scared schoolboys and had developed a technique for putting them at ease. He certainly did that for me and enabled me to retrieve my stomach into its proper place. Dr Harrison gave me my chance and I was offered a place at the university, subject of course to my 'A' level results. Under these conditions Sheffield looked a much different sort of place on the return trip to the station. You see, it's all a question of your state of mind, of how you want to view things. In the three succeeding years I grew with Sheffield. I was there when the last tram made its last journey. I saw many of the old bomb sites converted into bright new buildings, and by the time I stood on the steps of the City Hall in 1963 with my Bachelor of Engineering Degree in my hand, the city and its surrounds had burnt themselves a place of affection in my soul. I wouldn't have wished to have gone anywhere else to have taken my degree.

As I left the M1 motorway, which had not been in existence when I was at university, the 'burnt-in' affection for Sheffield as I passed through Attercliff and Pitsmoor was submerged for the time being, and I felt that old feeling of foreboding, more akin to the first day I visited the city. I drove through the thriving modern city centre but the phoenix didn't make its usual impact on me. I was on my way to another interview with a university don, and could feel in my bones that this one was to be one of those infrequent crossroads in life. Sometimes we are over them before we recognise them, but this one, to me, was clear. Professor Stewart was the traffic signal marking the crossing. He would caution me to take care and advise me on the direction, but it was still up to me to keep on or turn aside.

I parked in the car park next to the Students' Union on Western Bank. As it was Saturday afternoon there was plenty of room. I crossed the dual carriageway noting that the central reservation had been concreted in, whereas in my day it was planted with flowers and was a source of continual irritation because of impatient students trampling them down. The old university building hadn't changed much at all with its façade of red brick covered with ivy, now at its best in its autumn finery.

I climbed the stone steps to the porter's lodge and was directed up to the first floor. I passed Firth Hall and its memories of exams and all those elusive equations hiding among the cracks and crevices of the ceiling. The corridors still had the stamp of Victoriana with their high ceilings and musty echoes. I found the professor in his office in the wing overlooking the Western Park, in fact in exactly the same office he had occupied years ago. There was no Secretary on a Saturday afternoon and a tentative knock on the inner office door produced an immediate shout from inside.

"Come in."

I had caught Professor Stewart daydreaming or perhaps thinking deeply. He had a comfortable, old, green leather desk chair which swivelled, and he was leaning about as far back as the chair would go, with his feet up on one of those low two-drawer filing cabinets. He was facing the window, and it was quite obvious to me that this was a favourite contemplative position. He forced himself with obvious reluctance to consider who it was that had broken into his reverie.

"Good afternoon, Professor Stewart, I'm Tim Drummond. I wrote to you. I—"

"Of course." He came back to reality. "I'm so sorry, but I didn't recognise you."

"It would be surprising if you did, Professor, after seventeen years."

He nodded in agreement. "True, but I do like to think that I have a good memory. . ." – he pulled up a comfortable armchair in front of his desk as he was talking – ". . and I do remember you, even if I don't recognise you."

"You *do*?" I was a little surprised.

"Yes." He waved me to sit down. "Most lectures, you see, are pretty routine, but then occasionally something happens and it cuts its own distinctive memory niche. You, I remembered as soon as your letter jogged my memory." He picked up a paper clip and began unconsciously to fashion it into strange shapes. "To be honest with you, I expected to have heard about you or from you again *before* now."

"But why?" I was astounded.

He shook his head. "First of all, Mr Drummond, your letter didn't tell me very much about *why* you have at last come to see me. Perhaps a suitable starting point would be for you to tell me why you are here today."

He sat back comfortably, picking up a rule and winding the paper clip around it. "Don't hurry, I've plenty of time today."

Well, Professor Stewart, let me tell you what happened here in your lecture. . ." and once again I recounted my experiences. I wasn't interrupted at all. The professor nodded his head once or twice almost absent-mindedly, as though he already knew this story. Then I went on to my visit to Fountains Abbey and his fingers stopped their nervous working as his interest was caught and deepened. He refrained from comment right through my description of the Roman soldier at Housesteads. I stopped talking and waited for comment.

None was forthcoming immediately; it was almost as though my words had induced a trance. I restrained my impatience and waited. Suddenly his fingers began working the paper clip again. It snapped and that seemed to bring him back to earth. He looked at it for a moment and then tossed it into his waste bin. He took off his glasses and carefully placed them on the green tooled leather top of his desk and looked directly at me.

"Mr Drummond," he started, ". . .no, if you don't mind, I'll call you Tim."

I nodded in agreement and he carried on.

"Have you come here for answers, or for guidance?"

"Well, if you have them I'd like the answers, but I don't really think you will have, so I'd be grateful for some guidance."

"Good." He smiled, his hands now clasped together quietly in front of him.

"You looked at that old brain of mine all grey and gnarled, swirling around in its old preservative and it had a remarkable effect on you. I actually watched you that day and watched you hypnotise yourself—"

"*Hypnotise*?" I interrupted.

"Okay. . ." – he lifted his index finger in acknowledgement of my surprised question – ". . .perhaps *hypnotise* is the wrong word, but for now it will do until we find one more exact. I was fascinated because before I became interested in my present work, for a time I was a practising doctor of medicine. That old brain has fascinated me for years. I've always thought to myself, why is it so big? We don't use it all, so what's it all about? I've kept that old brain in my lecture theatre all these years to remind me of that question. However, there is only so much time in one's life and some things never get the attention they need to resolve the questions. One day, I've promised myself time and time again, I'll get down to trying to resolve the problem of that old brain. I watched you seventeen years ago, Tim, and thought that some answers were going to come. I thought that you would force my attention to the old brain – force me to really consider what is inside the cortex. But. . ." – he shook his head and smiled wistfully – ". . .you shook your head and came back to normal after a quarter of an hour and forgot about my problem."

"Until now, Professor."

"Yes, Tim, until now. Now it's your problem as well and we have to try to solve it." His eyes had a new sparkle. "In three years I will retire. Do you realise that my working life is virtually over and I was beginning to look forward to retirement, and now you've walked in from. . . from where, Tim? From the past, or from the future?

Perhaps my best work is still to be done!" His eyes suddenly clouded at my non-reaction. "Tim, you *are* going to look into this thing, aren't you?" I had been somewhat astounded at the professor's reaction. He had taken me completely seriously and in fact seemed almost to have expected me.

"Certainly, Professor, I had intended following it through, and I had hoped for your advice, but it sounds as though I've given you a new research project." I laughed and he laughed, the cloud lifting from his eyes.

"So, Professor, where do we start?"

"Let's walk along to my lecture theatre, Tim. That's the place it all started, so let's start from there."

We walked along the corridor and up to the second floor, our footsteps sounding hollow in that Saturday emptiness of a large building. We paused at the door of the lecture theatre numbered S214. The professor opened it and stopped in. I followed and stepped back in time – seventeen years.

Little had changed. Only the man walking down the steps in front of me, and then it was only his hair and beard. His hair was now a distinguished snowy white, whereas it had been grey-black, and his beard was now grey in place of the ginger mat which it had been then.

He stopped in front of his specimens. There it was, the old brain. For how many years had it slopped around in the yellowing bottle? A constant reminder to the professor about an unsolved question from his youth.

"You said in your letter that you worked in instrumentation and control, didn't you?"

"Yes, that's correct." I nodded.

"Do you have anything to do with computers at the moment?"

Again I nodded. "Yes, we install computers as part of chemical plant process control systems—"

"Tell me," he interrupted, "what size of computer are you working with at the moment?"

"Well, it's got 192K of memory, and discs, of course."

"Let's forget the discs for the moment," he mused. "One hundred and ninety-two thousand words of memory, and think of the space that that occupies – a couple of cards in nineteen-inch racking? He raised an inquisitive eyebrow.

I nodded.

"When you were here at university, that would have taken up more than fifty times that space. Technology is moving at a tremendous pace with electronics becoming more and more miniaturised, and it will go on getting smaller with memories becoming more and more powerful. But look, look at that old brain. It's already got that power. It's had it for thousands of years. What did you say it weighed?" The question was rhetorical: he was working through his fascination of the years. He put his thick black-rimmed glasses on again to see the brain more clearly. "Three and a half pounds it weighs, and it contains ten million nerve cells. Think of it, Tim, ten million nerve cells." He turned to me. "What do you know about the brain, Tim?" I pulled my eyes away from the old bottle.

"Very little more than that, I'm afraid."

"For years it has been traditionally assumed that man used his brain in a linear and sequential mode, taking one thought at a time and processing it. But, in fact, it is now apparent that our minds don't normally work in that way. They think in images, in key words and linked patterns, making use of most of our different senses. Similar, in fact, to a modern random access memory in a computer. I'm convinced that many of our problems in the past have been due to forcing our minds to work in a so-called logical sequence. If we recognise that every piece of information in our mind has many hooks and that these hooks can link up spatially in many directions, our brain power immediately becomes conceptually much larger." He stopped suddenly. "Sorry, I'm lecturing you."

"Don't worry about that. I really do want to know and I'm quite fascinated. So do go on." And so he did, developing his argument about hooks making interconnections in many directions. In fact, to put some incomprehensible scale onto them there were, he said, ten million neurons, every one capable of making more patterned interconnections than there are atoms in the universe. Each neuron has a tremendous choice of interconnections that it can make, and it makes these connections on the basis of stimulus, experience, and expectation. The Professor wasn't lecturing to me, he was revising his own thoughts about the brain, and strangely he had slipped unconsciously into a soft highland Scots' burr, not usually in evidence when he was lecturing.

"...if a brain becomes very busy and becomes involved in more complicated activity, the individual neurons grow more connections and the brain becomes more and more dense."

"You mean that the more I work my brain, the more it becomes capable of doing?"

"Yes, that's it exactly. Most people don't use their brains very well at all. In fact..." – he was warming to the subject now and had moved across to his desk and sat down – "...our very cultures encourage us not to use our brains to their full capability. We in the West place emphasis on logic and mathematics. As a general statement, this is dealt with by the left-hand side of our brain. Its concern and aptitude is with language and numbers, criticism and analysis. These are the things our society regards as important. The right-hand side, on the other hand, deals with rhythm, colour, dreams, spatial awareness and imagination. These are the facilities most prized in the East."

I nodded, catching the point he was making. "So that we don't develop our spatial awareness very well in our general life and they don't develop their logic."

Almost as though I hadn't spoken, Professor Stewart carried on.

"The result of that particular phenomena is really quite similar. *We* end up with slums and a poor quality of life because of lack of imagination, and *they* end up with slums and starvation amidst the beauty of buildings like the Taj Mahal, because they haven't the logic."

"It's a pity we couldn't put the two together, isn't it?"

"That is more *precisely* the point I'm making, Tim. Just think if we were able to develop both halves of the brain and get them to communicate. Because of this interlinking facility, our brain power would not merely be doubled, it would be many many times greater."

His enthusiasm was infectious and my earlier feelings of foreboding had almost entirely disappeared. I wasn't, however, quite prepared for where the professor was turning our thoughts next.

"When we have an idea, you know, it is just a new linking of neurons, a connection which had never been made previously. Once made, however, we usually find ourselves wondering why we never thought of it before. Most of the very important inventions or great leaps forward in human history have been conceptually simple. Well, here's one for you, Tim." He took off his thick black spectacles and waved them excitedly at me.

"If you could increase brain power tremendously by getting the left and right halves to communicate extensively, what increase in power could you obtain by getting two full brains to communicate together?"

He waited while I digested the question and its implications.

"Do you mean through telepathy?"

"Well, I'm not quite sure what I mean. But not the conventionally held view of telepathy. That always assumes a sequential use of a form of communications channel. To assume that would impose a similar misunderstanding to that already imposed on the single brain, and only recently overcome. No, you have to assume a sort of global means of communication, a means of extending the individual hooks of the neurons to cause interconnections with neurons in another brain."

I took a deep breath. "Certainly if that was possible, I can see that that would bring a vast increase in brain power, especially when you extend it to more than two brains."

We digested that powerful thought together until the professor suddenly exclaimed, "Goodness, look at the time. It's half past one! I have to be in town at two. Look, Tim, I'm sorry we've taken rather longer than I anticipated, and I don't think that so far I've helped you very much, have I?"

"Mmm," I mused. "Not really, you've given me plenty to think about, but I don't think I'm any further forward."

"Okay, so go away, have a wander around Sheffield, think about what we've said, and come back to see me at about five o'clock – I should be free by then. Can you do that?"

I readily agreed because I had a feeling that the crossroads were about me and that I had to make some decision today. The only problem was that the decision I needed to make wasn't clear and perhaps some more time with the professor would bring it into focus.

"Right, I'll see you at five o'clock then." His voice had resumed its normal standard English and he seemed unaware of the transition.

"Can you find your way out?"

"Yes, thank you."

We walked to the stairs together and he turned off to his office and I continued down to the tiled entrance foyer and out onto Western Bank.

I decided that the first stop would be for some lunch, and I decided to walk into town rather than catch a bus. I automatically walked down Hounsfield Road past the physics block and across the traffic lights at the bottom into Hanover Street. As a matter of curiosity, I walked down a couple of hundred yards to see if my old digs were still there. Sure enough, there it stood. I remembered being moved out of there when my landlady moved, because it was due to be knocked down to make room for a new ring road. It seemed as though this particular ring road had got lost.

I wandered into the town centre and had a reasonable steak and chips for lunch, but a town centre didn't suit the mood that Professor Stewart had induced in me, and I was soon out again by the simple expedient of jumping on a bus bound for Eccleshall.

I jumped off it again at Hunters Bar, and crossed the road to have a walk and while some time away in Endcliffe Park. I well remembered all the Sunday afternoons I had spent walking along through this park which was part of the Round-the-City walk. I walked along the stream side, fascinated by the water burbling and splashing cheerfully on its way to join the Donn. Before long I was through the park and across the road into Whitely Woods. Here it was peaceful, and my mood was matched by the late afternoon sun seeping through the leafless trees and glinting on the stream as it foamed over rocks and through miniature rapids and waterfalls. The sound was hypnotic as I went over and over again what the professor had talked about during the morning.

"Tim!" I was startled out of my reverie. Vaguely aware of someone approaching from ahead, I focused my eyes and was surprised to see Professor Stewart.

"You have an appointment at five." He pointed to his watch. I looked to find that it was already half past four. The afternoon had sped by in thought.

"Sorry, Professor. Looks like we're both going to be late." We laughed. I turned and fell into step beside him as we retraced our steps towards the university.

"You've saved me from being late, as well. Let's sit on that seat for a few minutes. I'm sure we can get through what we need to do here, and it really is much more pleasant at the moment."

We headed for the seat situated at a vantage point where the stream gurgled out into a pond full of ducks intent on standing on their heads in the water.

"Well, have you thought about what I said this morning?"

"I have, yes, but I'm afraid my hooks aren't connecting very well. It was all very interesting but where does it get me?"

We sat on the seat and Professor Stewart settled himself before answering.

"I don't want to rush the process, Tim. I believe that we. . . – he paused a moment – ". . .no, I don't mean we, I really mean *you*." He shook his head, a little sadly I thought. "*You* are on the brink of something very important, and it is very important that you yourself think it out, with perhaps a little help." He gazed out over the pond and to the ducks gasping for air. "The key to the inner processes of your mind is a particular state of consciousness. In that state, problems previously insoluble in the normal state of consciousness become soluble. You somehow have achieved, two or three times now, this state of mind – or very close to it. The way ahead, to me, is clear. We have to be able to induce your mind to this state, at will. We have to find the first key. When a brain does something automatically, it routes its connections along well-worn paths, it knows what to do. When it does something original, a new path is created. A flash of intuition is a connection between two neurons not previously made. You have formed these paths, but not consciously, and for some reason the paths are lost or hidden. We have to try to tread them again and mark the way for the future."

My crossroads were now standing out clearly. The professor sounded as though he was prepared to go with me into the unknown path which leads through the brain. But the other path also stood out. The other alternative was to ignore the mysteries of the brain and continue a normal life as an Instrument Engineer. That road was fairly clearly sign-posted. The turning, on the other hand, led to an unknown misty world. The way would be exciting and strange and might provide the new signposts for other people to follow.

"Tim, I'd like to know more about these strange happenings. If you are willing, I'd like to carry out a few experiments. What do you say?"

The time for decision was here, and in a flash of intuition my decision was taken and the crossroads were behind me.

I drew a deep breath. "Okay, Professor, let's take your path. What do you want to do?"

He smiled and his eyes flashed with happiness. He too was youthful again, but it was getting chilly as the sun had slipped away to look for someone else's day.

"Come on, let's walk. If we are going into this together, you must call me Jim."

"Okay, Jim it is." Jim it might be, but somehow I always thought of him as the professor rather than Jim.

"I've been thinking about this during the afternoon and what I would like to do is establish what conditions bring about your state of mind when this thing happens. So far we know the university, Fountains Abbey, and Housesteads. I don't see a link in all three yet, but Fountains and Housesteads are both ancient sites. Look around North Yorkshire, Tim, it's littered with abbeys, ruined and otherwise. Let's take a first stab at this problem. Next Saturday let's pay a visit to one of them. Have you a preference?"

For some reason I didn't have to think about it. It came straight out. "Let's try Rievaulx Abbey."

Chapter Five
Another Meeting – at Rievaulx Abbey

The professor and I had parted in Whitely Woods and had agreed to meet on the Saturday of the next weekend. We agreed to meet at about twelve o'clock in the Market Place at Helmsley. I returned to work on the Monday morning, very impatient for the week to pass and to get on with the experiment. It seemed that I wasn't the only one. As I got into the lift to go to the second floor I was accompanied by Bob Atwell, who had just dashed down the corridor to catch up with me.

"Well, Tim, did you see your professor?"

"Good morning, Bob."

"Sorry! Okay, good morning. Now did you see your professor?" There was no putting Bob off this morning without offending him.

"I did, yes."

"And so, what are we going to do next?" We got out of the lift at the second floor and I took in Bob's assumption that he would be involved.

"Aren't you going to tell me then?" he asked in a jaunty impish way, but with just the faintest trace of anxiety that I wasn't going to tell him. I managed not to tell him and he turned off into his office, but I'd barely reached my own and taken off my coat when he followed me in, rolling up his shirt sleeves.

"Right, Drummond." His red-faced smile belied his belligerent voice. "If you don't want to tell me, I'm not bothered, you know."

I gave in. "Okay, Bob, I'll tell you what happened, but I suggest you get a coffee and come and sit down."

And so I told him what the professor had said and about the planned visit to Rievaulx the following weekend.

He sat still for a few minutes when I'd finished and then, sitting straight in the chair, he said, "You might be wanting some help. I'm not doing anything on Saturday. I'm not kidding now, Tim. . . - he was unusually serious - ". . .you need someone to go with you who knows you. Have you anyone else who could do it?"

I had to admit that there wasn't really, not at such short notice anyway.

"Okay, Bob, I'm meeting the professor in Helmsley market place at about twelve o'clock. Can you get there for then?"

"Yes, no problem at all. Is there anything we need to take with us?"

"Since we don't know what we are doing yet, I think all we can take is ourselves."

I must say that I felt much happier to be going into this adventure with the solid practical support of Bob Atwell. There might be many problems ahead that a down-to-earth man like Bob might be better at solving than the academic Professor Stewart.

The week took its steady course, but I didn't feel to be all that frustrating. We had a large project on the go and it was a busy week. From time to time I was even able to forget about what we were going to do, but only for a time, and it usually came back to me with breathtaking, heart-stopping jolts, which left me tense with a sort of suppressed excitement.

By Saturday morning this tension had caught and held me tightly. I was awake early and had had breakfast and cleared away by eight o'clock. Four hours still until I would meet the others in Helmsley. It was only an hour's drive so I didn't need to leave until eleven, but by nine thirty I was impatient and itching for some action, so I decided to go, and instead of taking the direct route up Sutton Bank I would go by way of Kilburn, Byland, and Ampleforth.

The road up Sutton Bank is the main road and is a fast road giving the vast grand views from the top of the bank across the plain of York to the distant Pennine range, and later the stretches of bleak moorland between the top of the bank and Helmsley. The road which I took, on the other hand, running several miles further to the south, was a narrow winding road with continually changing views, mainly of well-cultivated valleys and dales. Whenever I travelled in this part of Yorkshire, I always recognised it as home and it had a soothing, restful effect on me. This Saturday was no different. I stopped for a while near to Byland Abbey, yet another of the many Yorkshire Abbeys with its lonely west front pointing to the sky. By the time I drove over the little hump-back bridge into Helmsley at about half past eleven, much of my tension had evaporated along with the morning frost as the sun climbed into the winter blue sky.

Helmsley is a little North Yorkshire town, which in the summer gets more tourists than it can comfortably cope with, but off-season it is very pleasant. There was plenty of parking places in the square and I parked immediately in front of the market cross. A quick look around the square convinced me that the professor hadn't yet arrived, nor had Bob Atwell. Still it was a long journey from Sheffield, and if I had been Bob I would have come via the Great Broughton Moor road and stopped for a quarter of an hour to enjoy the views from the top of Rievaulx Moor across towards Hawnby Moor. I contained my impatience and had a wander around Helmsley in the morning sunshine, looking in the windows of the new little shops which seemed to be popping up everywhere – pottery, antiques, dress shops, and so on. They did not intrude into this pleasant town. Some care had been taken to blend them into the peaceful, lazy atmosphere of the town. They shyly peered from little alleyways and occasionally apologised for being on the main road.

I spotted Professor Stewart as he backed into the space between my car and a white Ford Escort. I was at his elbow almost before he could get out of the car.

"Good morning, Professor, you've made it spot on time." The church clock had just commenced to strike midday.

"Yes, not bad, eh? Good morning, Tim. By Jove, it really is a good morning here too, isn't it?" He breathed in deeply the North Yorkshire air.

"Do you know anywhere for a reasonable lunch?" He reached into the car for his overcoat.

I was taken aback as I'd not thought about that.

"Tim, I've been on the road for two and a half hours and I need sustenance before anything. You do too. Come on, there's a little café on the corner over there." He took my arm and guided me towards a little shop with a bow window.

"Just a minute, Professor." I'd caught sight of Bob Atwell pulling into the square.

"I hope you don't mind, but I've asked a colleague of mine from work to come with us."

"Not at all. I thought after you left last week that it would be better if we had someone else with us."

We walked over to greet Bob as he got out of his car, and I introduced them.

"Please, please call me Jim, not Professor." Professor Stewart shook hands and pointed to the café. "We were just heading over there for a spot of lunch, if you've no objections, before we start today's proceedings."

"No objections at all, Jim. In fact, that'll suit me fine. I've had no breakfast today. . ." – he patted his stomach – ". . .so I can forget my slimming menu today."

The café, which in the summer would swarm with day-trippers, was not very full and it had a roaring wood fire in the grate. It served an excellent home-made steak and kidney pie with the usual chips and peas. This was preceded by a thick soup which wasn't out of a tin and was followed by a fruit flan, again home-made, and by the time we reached coffee we were very comfortable indeed. Like the fire which had settled down nicely to a comfortable red glow, we felt more like settling down in front of it for a chat.

However, we three had met to visit Rievaulx Abbey, and so, after paying the very reasonable bill, we all piled into the professor's car and took the B1257 road from the north-west corner of the square. Two miles out of town we took the left turn down through the avenue of trees and through the narrow village street to turn into the Abbey car park.

We parked, and as I got out of the car that comfortable feeling engendered over our pleasant lunch disappeared completely and my stomach muscles knotted themselves again.

Rievaulx Abbey, like Fountains, was founded by the Cistercians, but unlike the very solid structure of Fountains, it is built in the early English style of architecture with its three tiers of arcading to the north and south of the presbytery and quire, and a double tier of three lancets at the east end. Everything in the structure carries the eyes to the heavens and lifts the soul from the everyday. It wasn't the first time that I had visited Rievaulx Abbey, and both the professor and Bob had been before. As we paid our entry fee at the gate and walked towards that massive structure of stone and light I wondered again what sort of men they had been who had picked out this lovely sheltered spot in the Rye Valley. Had they a keen eye for the loveliest prospects and richest bits of land, or was it because of their industry and work over several hundred years that they had turned the area into what it now is?

We walked into the building by the north transept and, standing under the great tower arch, looked along the quire to the east. The atmosphere engendered by those centuries-old ruins had been stealing over us as we strolled aver the grass to the building and now quietly standing, surrounded by it, it soaked over and into us. Bob Atwell was first to speak.

"Okay, Tim. We're here now, what do we do?"

I, in turn, turned to the professor. "Well, Professor, do you know what we are to do?"

Jim Stewart took out his thick black rimmed spectacles from their case but didn't put them on. He brought his eyes down from the lofty peaks. He produced a little grunt and scratched his grey beard in contemplation.

"I don't *know* what we are to do, Tim, but let's feel our way slowly. Let's recap for a moment." He leaned his back against one of the fluted columns of the arch.

"We have to find what is the key to the newly active part of your brain, Tim. We've come to Rievaulx because it is not dissimilar to Fountains, and if my theory in right we can create a similar effect here."

"Sorry, Professor," Bob was adopting my way of addressing Jim Stewart, "what *is* your theory? I didn't know you had one."

A slow smile broke over the professor's face. "Look, you two, I don't want to tell you just at the moment until we've tried it out."

"But look—" I protested, but was stopped short by the professor.

"I *promise*, whatever the outcome this afternoon, I'll tell you. Okay?"

I nodded, not entirely happy, but I wanted to get on with it. It was now two o'clock and there was just the hint of a lengthening of the shadows around us, cast by the wintry sun.

"The weather conditions aren't quite as you described at Fountains, Tim." It was more of a statement than a question and he never waited for me to answer.

"I think that doesn't matter too much, though. It was perhaps important to produce an accidental trigger to the mind, but this time you are consciously going to try triggering this experience. What I do believe *is* important is quiet and peace and concentration. I don't think there is anyone else here this afternoon apart from us three and the gateman, so we have the conditions. Bob and myself will stay here and I want you to walk slowly, very slowly, along the centre of the ruins, towards the high altar. Try to relax, put everything out of your mind, and try to open it to—"

"To what, Professor?"

"That, Tim, I don't know. Are you ready?"

I took a deep breath and nodded.

"Good luck, Tim." Bob patted my shoulder. Gone was the usual cheerful banter. He was deadly serious and anxious now. Strangely enough, as I parted from them and stood in the centre of the arch, my own earlier anxieties had drained away. The knots in my stomach had been loosened and I concentrated on the peak of the centre lancet window, framing a still clear blue November sky.

I took a step forward, slowly and carefully. For a moment I heard a car engine rev as it turned into the car park below us, but I managed successfully to exclude it from my conscious mind. There was no wind eddying around me today as I paced slowly forward. My mind was programmed to the source of action and the motor senses took over and controlled my movements as I drew level with the second arch. Somehow it was easier than I had envisaged, this emptying of my mind to everyday happenings and events. By the time I had reached the high altar the white sandstoned arches about me had merged into the sky about them. Their majestic lifting pillars had done their job and lifted me out of myself. I felt myself stop, in the eye of that religious building, at the high altar. For some reason I closed my eyes and my breathing reduced to the merest whisper of air. There were no external sounds from the wintry valley around us to distract me. I forgot about the two men waiting anxiously under the arch. In my mind's eye I could still see the lancet window in front of me, pointing and leading me to the heavens.

Suddenly it came. One instant it wasn't there, the next it was. It was there as though it had always been there, and perhaps it had. The sound I had heard years ago in Sheffield, but somehow not quite the same. Then, I hadn't been expecting it; this time I was looking for it but without knowing what I was looking for. I recognised, without any fear of being mistaken, that throbbing, pulsing stream of energy. In Sheffield it had beaten at me and vibrated in pulsing undirected power, and again at Fountains the power had been unfocused and had come in random waves, tumbling and crashing around me. Now I could feel it – a pure stream of clear, bright, sharp energy searing its way through my brain.

My brain? Yes, that wasn't too clear at first. Where was this energy stream? I could see it, feel it all around me, but was it in the church? I didn't think so. No, I was positive that it was more personal than that. It wasn't about me really. It was inside me, giving me a feeling of immense security and knowledge. I felt that I could reach out back through the ages and know everything that had happened from the dawn of creation. I didn't, but I knew that if I wanted to, I could. The feeling of confidence and security which that knowledge gave me was overwhelming. This tingling stream of razor-sharp energy was singing its way through well-worn channels of stored information, renovating it, bringing it up to date, and adding new knowledge. It continually sorted it, identified it in packages, and restored it, perhaps in a new place, a better place, a place for easier access. All that I'd ever learnt was there. Not forgotten at all. It was all stored in a vast library of information which I just had to open at will. But there was more, surely? Yes, *infinitely* more. No way had I ever learnt or read about this much information and knowledge. The awareness was tremendous, but now there was something else reaching into the stream of energy. Like a pinpoint of light flashing through the air to join the stream. Not of the stream, but something new. I couldn't feel where it had come from. Then another and another. Now there was a flickering intermittent smaller stream of consciousness. But where? I strove to locate the source of this new energy, which had its own clear signature. It was worried, uncertain, and I reached out to reassure it and then it made contact. But the effect of that contact was cataclysmic. The new energy source shrieked fear at me and was instantly gone. I felt my new-found energy stream wavering and a profound sense of sadness and loss unsettled me. The sharpness was going: it was dimming and wavering. Slowly but definitely it receded from me. The bulkheads of time descended and locked themselves automatically, and I became aware that my knees were hurting and my legs too. I opened my eyes to find myself kneeling back on my heels. The first thing I saw was the lancet window. Strangely though, the blue sky had gone and white, scudding clouds chased their way across it. The sounds of the world about me also impinged on my ears. It was only a wind funnelling up the church. But it was darker as well. The sun had gone and with it that pleasant November day which I had excluded a few moments before. I tried to stand up but fell, flat on my face.

Almost immediately there were sounds about me of running feet and I was turned onto my back to see the anxious strained faces of Professor Stewart and Bob Atwell.

It seemed that they obviously hadn't expected to find me conscious because their surprise was clear.

"Tim, are you okay?"

"I think so, Bob – if you can pull me up."

"But you've just collapsed, shouldn't you—?"

"Just pull me up. My legs have gone to sleep, that's all. Though how they go to sleep standing for a few minutes beats me."

They glanced quickly at each other as I was pulled into a sitting position.

"I'm not surprised they've gone to sleep, Tim." The professor spoke gently with his Highland Scot's accent. "You may not realise it, but you've been kneeling for the last *two* hours, and apart from sinking back onto your heels about three quarters of an hour ago, you've *not* moved."

I wasn't too surprised at this information because I remembered the time I'd lost at Fountains Abbey.

"Come on, you two, pull me up." The blood returning to my legs was giving me hell and I had to be supported on each side.

"We were starting to get worried about you, Tim." Bob had recovered himself again. "We were just discussing how we could bring you round when that girl walked in and seemed to break you—"

"*What* girl?" I looked around quickly, but there was no one to be seen. Both the professor and Bob looked around too.

"She came in over there, about halfway down the north side," said the professor, pointing.

I could hear a car engine coughing into life in the car park. "Quick, I want to see that car." Half crippled or not, I pulled my puzzled supports with me until I could see the car park. Sure enough, I had known what I would see. A white Ford Escort was pulling out of the car park. It rapidly disappeared from sight into the village and soon it could only be heard labouring up the hill on the other side.

Chapter Six
Post-Mortem

"Damn!" I exclaimed, "she's gone again."

"Interesting, *very* interesting." The professor was nodding sagely to himself.

"Would you two mind telling me what's going on?" Bob was going red with curiosity.

"The girl from Fountains Abbey?" The professor had a habit of making questions into incontrovertible statements.

"It would be too much of a coincidence, wouldn't it, if she isn't?"

"Look, Bob, come on, let's get back to the car and drive into Helmsley. There's just a chance that she'll go there."

"But why?" Bob was bursting, but nevertheless we set off back to the car.

"Because she's frightened," I explained.

"Frightened? How do you know?"

"Did you make contact with her, Tim." The suppressed excitement in the professor's voice came through the quietly-put question.

"Yes, but... well, not exactly. I can't really explain what happened, but I think I made a contact, but she wasn't prepared for it and I felt the echo of her shock. That's how I know she's frightened."

We walked passed an indifferent gatekeeper intent only on watching the clock tick around to four thirty when he could padlock his cabin and go home to the television.

We settled back in the professor's comfortable car and with the engine running it wasn't long before some warmth began to seep back into me. I hadn't realised until I'd got back into the car how cold I was and how my teeth were chattering.

"I think we ought to get him home to bed," said an anxious Bob.

"No." I was firm.

"No, Bob. I don't think it's shock. A warm drink and a nice fire will soon warm him through and then we can have a talk about what happened." At last a hint of curiosity had burst out of the professor. So far it had all been concern that I was okay. But now that that seemed to be settled so, let's get back to the experiment. Now was the time to study the results and see if any conclusions could be drawn.

At about five o'clock we were back in Helmsley market place and parked in front of the Black Swan. I looked around the square but the Escort was nowhere in evidence.

"Come on, let's go into the Black Swan. It looks the sort of place we might find a good old-fashioned fire." I agreed with Jim Stewart and followed his lead into the hotel. Sure enough, he was right. In the grate of the old beamed lounge overlooking the square was a nice coal fire crackling away to itself.

While Bob and I warmed ourselves through in the traditional way with our backs to the fire, Professor Stewart went to find someone in the apparently deserted hotel to bring us some hot drinks. He came back with a happy smile.

"Right, hot tea is on the way and..." – he turned to Bob – "...how much time have you got, Bob?"

"Oh, as much as you want. I've had my pass signed for the full day today."

"Good. I've ordered dinner for half past seven and I hope you will be my guests." He pulled an armchair close around the fire and we followed suit.

"Right, Tim, now let's hear your story please."

"It's very difficult, you know."

"Yes, I expected it would be, but concentrate. Let's have as much as you can remember please."

It really was difficult to remember what had happened at first, but as I recounted my feelings and tried to relive my experience it became easier. For half an hour I stared into the flickering flames of the fire and drank the scalding hot tea as I recounted the tale. No one interrupted me. For minutes at a time there was total silence as I strained to remember and continue. I got up from time to time to pace around the room and stare out of the window across the darkening square.

That was where I completed my story, straining to see a white Ford Escort. I was joined as I finished by Professor Stewart.

"I'm sorry, Tim. I wish I had been quick enough to put two and two together and realise that it was the girl who had brought you round."

"It wasn't your fault, Professor," said Bob. "If you remember, we hardly noticed the girl. It was Tim falling flat on his face that we were more concerned with."

"That's true, Bob, that's true. . . Come and sit down, Tim. I'm afraid we are not going to see her this evening. Pity really, I only glanced at her, but from what I can remember she was quite attractive."

I accompanied him back to the fire and asked as he threw on some more coal from the scuttle, "Could you recognise her again?"

He thought for a minute. "Yes, I believe I could."

"I could as well."

"That might be more useful. If you can remember her, Bob, and if she's local, we might be able to find her." He laughed, stretching himself out in his chair, and said with an impish grin, "I hope that you are going to make my excuses to my wife when I go round staring at all good-looking blondes."

We laughed and the tension eased, and I sat down as the fire roared eagerly, going to work on its new load of black energy.

"Well, Professor, do you count the experiment a success or a failure, and where has it got us?"

"You were going to tell us what your theory was," prompted Bob.

"Let's start there then." Professor Stewart acknowledged Bob's question first.

"I thought about all of Tim's experiences and I came to the conclusion that they were triggered in different places for perhaps different reasons. He is obviously very susceptible to this experience and it only needs something quite minor to make him experience them. Sheffield was the first one. I tend to discount that one as sheer chance. Perhaps the hypnotism - of my voice, the atmosphere outside the lecture room, the presence of my old brain and so on. The next two are more interesting, however, as they both took place on old religious sites. So my theory was that for some reason, as yet unspecified, old religious sites were possibly nodes of resonance where this thing could happen."

"But," interrupted Bob, "one was Christian and one was at a pagan site."

"Does it matter?" The professor had found a paper clip from somewhere and was unconsciously bending it into the form of a cross. "Both religions worshipped God as each saw him. Let's face it, none of us, even those of us who profess to be Christians, really know what God is. The Romans worshipped Mithras, an ancient Persian god who was the Sun god, a warrior god fighting against the powers of darkness and evil on behalf of mankind. Incidentally, I've looked up a bit of information this week – I don't just happen to know this." The professor had pre-empted a question and continued. "The figures of Mithras portray him as a young man in Persian dress in the act of stabbing a bull with a dagger. This represented a mystical sacrifice performed on behalf of mankind and through which he obtained the triumph of good over evil and the ascent of the human soul to God. You can recognise that in this idea of sacrifice for mankind, it has something in common with Christianity."

"That's true," admitted Bob, and for a few moments we sat and digested the information, and then Bob took Professor Stewart's argument a little further.

"You know, when you think about it, though," he began his head cocking at an angle as he was half speaking to himself. "every religion does tend to get back to a basic belief that over and outside our world something or someone exists who is a superior being but who can and does influence events."

We agreed with that, but as yet I couldn't see where his argument was going.

"In fact, primitive man, when confronted with something mysterious or awe inspiring, was conscious of a stirring within him. Without forming any theories about it, he was aware of another world which had somehow burst into this world."

"I hadn't realised that you were a philosopher, Bob."

He grinned. "You see, I'm not just a thick engineer, Tim. But wait – joking aside, don't you think that these people realised that they had a need for something which the world was unable to provide. This need had to come from another world and was most easily expressed in terms of gods and sacred sites. In these sacred sites, his beliefs found expression in sacred action and rites which enabled him to establish communication with. . ." – he faltered for a moment –

". . .I was going to say God, but I'm not sure about that. Perhaps it was this other world or perhaps to commune with the rest of human society. . ."

"Or perhaps. . ." the professor picked up the theme, ". . .perhaps it was the universe in all its aspects."

Bob nodded. "Yes, though I'm not too sure that I understand what you are saying there. But the point I was trying to make is that Fountains and Rievaulx are just places where man has gathered to commune with this. . . this, well, let's call it God for now as we have to call it something. For centuries, men gathered and performed sacred rites and ceremonies and spent much time in deep contemplation, thinking about God. Perhaps in some way these places have become sounding boxes or resonance chambers for these thoughts and Tim is somehow able to tune into them."

I was startled. Here was the very pragmatic Bob Atwell descending (or possibly ascending) into the realms of science fiction, and I said as much to him.

"No, Tim, don't exclude what Bob is saying. We cannot at this point in time afford to ignore anything. You have to accept that something very strange happens to you and we need to explore all the possibilities."

"To keep an open mind in fact," emphasised Bob. I ignored the intended pun.

"But if what you've just said was true, what I experienced and described was happening to me from outside, not from inside me, but I am positive it came from within me."

"Okay, let's try this one for size before we go in to dinner. There could be some truth in what Bob is saying, but suppose, amidst all this contemplation which has gone on here, the human mind was able to not only commune with Bob's God, but also to know itself deeper. For some reason as yet unestablished, Tim found that he was better able to know himself."

"Yes. . . I'll accept that as well," conceded Bob, "but don't forget that we know he also communicated outside of himself. Don't forget the girl. Tim himself described some contact with her."

At that point the head waiter came in to take our order for dinner. Used to the leisurely choice and arguments that go on with most dinner parties, he was obviously surprised at the speed with which we selected from his menu. This time, however, he was dealing with a group more interested in arguing about the unknown than about menus. Selection having been dispensed with, the professor was first to break the contemplative silence which had descended upon us.

"You know, Bob," he pointed his forefinger at Bob emphasising that he was still continuing with Bob's previous point, "even if we accept that Tim did make contact outside of himself, which we are reasonably sure he did do in some sort of primitive way, my previous point is still valid. The fact is that if Tim was able to know himself better, part of this knowing might in fact provide the knowledge of how to contact other people."

Suddenly Bob's face split into a grin and he started laughing to himself. We looked at him, rather startled.

"Did I say something funny?"

"No, Professor, but it suddenly occurred to me that perhaps all those monks who went around with a vow of silence weren't giving anything up at all. They were still all secretly chattering among themselves using brain power." He sat, still cackling to himself, and we had a laugh too, but the professor's was more of the kind of courtesy laugh at someone else's joke. I felt that he thought that there might be some truth in it.

During the meal which followed, conversation was spasmodic as we thought about our pre-dinner conversation, and it wasn't until we were back in the lounge with after-dinner coffee that the conversation picked up properly again. The dinner wine had also mellowed us and perhaps loosened our tongues a little, but the essential point was that we did not get any further forward.

"Well, gentlemen." Bob sat up straight eventually. He indicated the clock and slapped his hands onto his knees. "It's nine thirty now. By the time I get back to Hartlepool it's going to be eleven o'clockish, so I think I'd better be going."

"But," I protested, "we haven't established what the next move is going to be yet."

"Well," replied Bob, "you two sort it out while I take a walk out the back to the Gents before I go." He got to his feet and disappeared through the lounge door.

"Can we determine what our next move is as quickly as that, professor?"

"Tim, the next move is in fact obvious to me. When I do experiments, I always repeat them to confirm their validity."

"You mean, you want to go into Rievaulx again?"

"In principle, yes. But it doesn't have to be Rievaulx. In fact, it would give it more validity if it wasn't Rievaulx. Let's say it ought to be another abbey. Let's see now. What if next week we went to—"

He broke off as Bob reappeared in the lounge door with a very excited look on his face.

"Tim, you've spent half the night looking out into the square for that white Ford Escort. It's been here all the time. It's in the car park at the back of the hotel."

"What! Are you sure it's the same one?" I never waited to hear the answer as I quickly followed Bob out of the door again. Professor Stewart was only half a step behind me too.

"There, over there."

There were two arc lights mounted on the yard walls which brightly lit up the car park.

Parked against the back walls, almost at the point where the two lights were focused, was a white Ford Escort. All the cars in the yard were thickly covered in frost and there weren't many tyre marks in the frost on the ground. I slithered over the yard.

"There aren't any tyre marks here. It looks as though it's been here all the evening." I examined the car and noted its registration number.

Bob, as practical as ever, said, "We're no further forward really. We never saw the registration of the one at Rievaulx, did we?"

"No, but we could check through the reception desk, couldn't we?" asked the professor.

"Good idea," Bob acknowledged. "Let's get back inside, it's bloody cold out here without a coat on." He'd forgotten that he was supposed to be going home now, and also that he had been going to go to the toilet.

We all marched back into the reception and as I rang the little brass call bell I was almost holding my breath.

"Yes, sir, can I help you?" the little dark-haired receptionist asked.

"I hope so. Look, here's a car number – can you tell us if it belongs to one of your guests?"

"Let's see, sir." She took the piece of paper and turned to her registration book. In a few moments she had checked. "Yes, sir, a Miss K. Bishop. Is she blocking your way out?"

I looked at her in some surprise. It was a few seconds before I realised that she thought the car was blocking our exit from the car park.

"No, not at all." The Professor was coming to the rescue.

"Is Miss Bishop in? Could I talk to her on the phone?" He pointed to the instrument on the desk.

A faintly suspicious look drifted across the girl's eyes now.

"Do you want to see her?"

"Yes, we really would like to see her." I supported the professor.

"Well, her key isn't here, so she may be in." The receptionist was still a bit doubtful about these three man who had appeared from nowhere and who didn't even know the name of the person they wanted to see. She lifted the telephone and glanced around, looking for possible help. She dialled a number which rang for several moments, but no one replied.

The door to the restaurant opened and help came for all of us. It was the head waiter with our bill.

"Mr Ryan, these three gentlemen are looking for Miss Bishop. Have you seen her?"

"Certainly I have. She's in the restaurant. Do you want to go through to her, Mr Stewart?"

We thanked the receptionist and followed Mr Ryan towards the restaurant door.

We stopped at the door. "Er, just a moment please. We don't want to spoil her meal. We will just wait until she's finished."

The waiter peered through the glass of the door. "Well, you'll not have to wait long, sir, she's onto her sweet now."

Bob had stepped up to the door and was following the waiter's eyes to a table by the right-hand wall of the restaurant.

"Perhaps you'd direct her into the lounge when she's finished," said Bob.

I was elated. He had obviously recognised the girl.

"Don't tell her we're there. It'll be a surprise for her." The professor knew that the waiter hadn't heard us asking the receptionist for her name, so he happily played along with us assuming we were friends of hers.

"No problem at all, sir. I'll serve her coffee there."

We all trooped back into the lounge again and reclaimed our seats around the now pleasantly glowing fire, and Bob pulled up another spare chair and put a coffee table near it.

"We have to get prepared, you know."

"What do you mean, *we*. Don't you realise it's getting on for ten o'clock. You should be on your way home," I pointed out.

"Blast," he muttered, staring at me for a moment. It didn't take him long to reach a decision. "I'll just go and make a phone call to Margaret. Looks like I'm going to be late, doesn't it?"

"Shall I phone for you and explain that you're late because you are waiting to chat up a blonde?"

"You would as well, wouldn't you?"

Bob had no sooner left the room than a waitress appeared with some coffee cups and coffee and put them down on the table which Bob had moved near to the fire. Our more friendly head waiter had thoughtfully provided us with coffee, as well as for Miss Bishop.

Bob was back quickly and had just sat down when Miss Bishop came into the room. I assumed that she was Miss Bishop, and Bob's slight inclination of his head confirmed it.

I spread out the cups and began to pour the coffee. The young lady was looking around a little uncertainly for her tray.

"I assume that you are looking for your coffee?" The professor caught her attention.

"I do believe they have included yours with ours. Perhaps you would like to join us around the fire?" He indicated the armchair pulled up so recently by Bob Atwell and skilfully placed so as to be a little separate from our chairs. It could then be either part of our grouping or not, as she pleased.

She appraised each of us carefully and then nodded.

"Thank you, it *is* a nice fire, isn't it? Just right for a cold night like tonight."

She took the coffee cup and saucer I held out to her. As I proffered the sugar, I took the opportunity to look at her again. As she carefully dug her spoon into the sugar bowl and measured out the grains to give a half spoon, I decided that she was probably about twenty-five or six. She wasn't the traditional picture that everyone thinks of when one talks of a beautiful blonde. Her long hair, pulled back with a material band, was more straw coloured than blonde and had rebelled at the attempt some time earlier this evening to brush it into shape. Her face, too long to be classical, was troubled by a slight frown which tended to pull her fair eyebrows together. As she put the sugar into her coffee she glanced up to say thank you, and the red fire light danced in her grey eyes, but the fire lights were deceptive and before she looked away again to sit back in her chair, I had realised that her eyes were troubled. She seemed to curl herself up in the chair, almost shrinking deeper into the thick blue high-necked sweater she was wearing, and tucking her feet under her legs, smoothing down the long grey heavy skirt, she stared into the glowing fire embers and settled down to ignore us completely.

"Miss Bishop?"

She was like a scalded cat as Professor Stewart spoke her name into the pool of ensuing silence broken only by an occasional crackle from the fire.

Her cup crashed to the saucer and her eyes leapt at the professor in fear.

"How do you know my name?" Her pleasant voice was taut, and the question was fired at close range almost in a whisper.

"Miss Bishop, please don't be afraid." We left it to Professor Stewart. After all, he more than ever, in the soft firelight, cast the father figure, a gentle father figure with his white hair and grey beard, almost like some of the Victorian figures portrayed in the prints hung around the hotel lounge.

He didn't answer her question directly but simply carried on talking.

"Please, I insist, *don't* be afraid." His voice had slipped into the soft gentle highland lilt. "We know that you are worried," he encompassed Bob and myself in his gesture, "and we would like to help you. No. . ." he mused, "that's not entirely true. We do want to help you, but at the same time we want *you* to help *us*."

Her initial shock at hearing her name from a complete stranger was subsiding, and she hadn't moved at all in her chair. She had now got a grip of herself and some control back into her voice and she did some insisting of her own.

"You haven't told me how you know my name."

"You were at Rievaulx Abbey this afternoon, weren't you?"

She gasped. "But how—"

"And unless I'm very much mistaken, you were at Fountains Abbey on the first Saturday in November."

Her head turned and, pushing back her rebellious straw-coloured hair, she took a long, cool, hard look at me.

I noticed that the worried frown had gone. It had been replaced by lines in her forehead, but they were lines of concentration. Eventually, after what seemed an age of silence she spoke again.

"It *was* you, wasn't it? It *was* you." Her relief was transparent. She put her two hands to her face and drew a deep, deep breath, held it for some moments and exhaled slowly. Her deep sigh whirled around our little pool of people and pulled us all together. With no more introduction she inexplicably accepted us as friends. We were over the difficult part. She might have screamed, she might have called the manager to have us flung out, she might have done anything, but before the head waiter poked his head around the door to see that all was okay she had released her spring of pent-up worry and her relief was all enveloping.

"Tell me," asked the professor before any introductions were made, "how did you know it was him?"

Miss Bishop smiled as she turned back to the professor and said simply, "Because our minds have just made contact again and I recognise him."

Chapter Seven
Kate

"Christ!" The exclamation was Bob's. I was amazed because I had felt no contact at all.

"Do you mean that you are able to mentally contact people at will?" The professor was first to formalise our whirling thoughts.

"No, I can't do that."

"But you've just said that your minds have made contact now and you recognise him."

"Yes, I did say that, didn't I, but it's the first time that something like that has happened."

It looked like being a long night. I took a deep breath and plunged in. "Before we get bogged down in theoretical discussion again we ought to introduce ourselves and I would suggest, Jim, that we perhaps ought to book ourselves into the hotel for the night."

"Hey, look, I can't do that." Bob was looking at his watch, torn between wanting to stay and the necessity to be getting off home.

"It's okay for these single men, Miss Bishop, but I'll have to introduce myself and leave." He stood up and stuck out his hand. "I'm Bob Atwell."

Miss Bishop uncurled a hand from the depths of her thick jumper and shook hands with him.

"Hello, Bob, please call me Kate – it's not quite so stuffy, is it?"

Bob continued with the introductions and introduced the professor who said, "Please call me Jim." Kate Bishop, however, did the same as the rest of us and called him Professor most of the time. He was just that sort of figure: it was more natural to call him Professor than Jim.

"And this chap is the source of all our troubles – Tim Drummond."

I leaned across and held out my hand to be shaken by hers, soft but confidently firm. Perhaps our hands stayed in contact for some moments longer than strictly necessary, but perhaps that was only to be expected after our strange mutual contact. Our eyes met grey to grey and tried to probe their respective depths, but though I tried I felt no further contact.

She shook her head and pulled a wry face. "No, Tim, I can't feel it now."

Our hands dropped apart and Bob interrupted. "I'm off then. I'll want a full report from you on Monday." Bob said goodnight to everyone and with a smile and a wave he pulled on his coat and disappeared.

It was about a quarter of an hour before we settled in around the dying fire embers again after booking in at Reception for the night. Throwing some logs on which had mysteriously appeared during our absence, the professor kicked off the conversation.

"I think that we can help each other, Kate. I'd like to think that after Tim has told you about his strange experiences you might be interested enough to join our experiment."

Kate Bishop had one of those transparent faces that reflected her thoughts though she was totally unaware of the fact. At the moment it reflected excitement, which was infinitely preferable to the naked fear that she had transmitted earlier. She was like a little girl waiting for a story. So I told her the story, simply, with no theories as to the whys and wherefores. She in turn told us that she was a teacher of English from Sheffield. From the start of the summer term she had moved to Northallerton and was teaching at Northallerton Grammar School.

"I had never visited any of the Yorkshire abbeys before so I decided to remedy that one weekend, and one Saturday afternoon I'd been to Ripon on some business. I finished early and thought it a good opportunity to spend a little time looking at Fountains Abbey."

She looked at me. "I went into the Abbey grounds thinking how few people there were around. That wasn't surprising of course because it was quite a stormy afternoon." She relinquished her hold on my eyes and looked into the flames now licking around her legs.

"I thought how magnificent the Abbey building was, standing apparently totally deserted in the valley. It wasn't until I entered the building by the main door that I realised there was someone else there. As I gazed along the ruined church I could see the figure of a man standing in the centre of the high altar. At first I'd thought he was another stone column. I remember what he was wearing now – a sort of sandstone coloured cord anorak. He was tall, probably about six foot two with a mop of thick black hair. I couldn't see more than that as he had his back to me, but it was his stillness that stopped me going in any further." She paused and collected together her recollections. No one interrupted her. She had a commanding way of speaking. She spoke softly but distinctly and with a pleasant South Yorkshire accent.

"I stood for some minutes waiting for him to move, but he didn't. His arms were folded and he was absolutely still. The wind was blowing all around me, but for some strange reason it hardly ruffled his clothes and hair. For about five minutes I watched and then I began to be a little afraid. I told myself not to be so silly and tried to calm myself. I was just beginning to succeed when I felt a presence – not a physical presence beside or near to me, but in my head. It was probing and I couldn't understand what it was and I became very frightened, and I decided that I'd had enough of Fountains Abbey. I ran nearly all the way back to the gate. As I went through, the gateman asked if there was anyone else, and I did tell him that was a man."

"I'm sorry, Tim, you might have been in terrible trouble, but I was scared and only wanted to be away from that place. Later, when I'd recovered, I felt guilty and wondered if that man. . . you. . . needed help. I read the local papers for days expecting to find some reference to a sick man or something, but there wasn't." She lapsed into a sort of regretful silence until prompted by the professor.

"And now to today, Kate. What happened today?"

"Today, Professor, was the first day that I've plucked up courage since then to visit an abbey again. What a difference in days. It was a beautiful afternoon, wasn't it?"

We confirmed that with nods.

"But it turned into the same nightmare again. I couldn't believe it. I walked into the church structure and I was aghast. There was the same man except that this time he was kneeling, no. . . he was sitting back on his heels, but absolutely still."

She shuddered a little at the remembered shock and unconsciously put out her hand and gripped mine tightly.

"The presence was there again. It wasn't evil, but it was doing things to my brain. I could feel the little shocks of contact and began to be afraid. Suddenly it became stronger and I felt a deep consciousness of contact, but I'd had enough and I was terrified. Once again I ran away." Her hand was tightening its hold and showing white across the knuckles.

"I drove like a maniac away from Rievaulx, and by the time I came down into Helmsley, reaction was setting in and I was trembling. I realised that I would never be able to drive back to Northallerton in that state so I booked into a room here for the night and went to bed for a few hours." She smiled a quick nervous smile. "And that's all until now, and suddenly, from nowhere, there's someone to tell it to. Someone who won't think I'm daft. Oh, I'm sorry. . ." She suddenly realised that she had been gripping my hand and let it go, rather embarrassed.

"Don't worry, Kate, feel free to grab my hand whenever you want." But nevertheless I rubbed my fingers. I wouldn't have expected her long fingers to be capable of such a vice-like grip.

"What does it mean, Professor? What's it all about?"

"I don't know, Kate, but we have one or two theories you might listen to." And he told her what we'd talked about up to now.

"So you see," he concluded, "we have had a good experiment today. The conclusions aren't too obvious."

"You can say that again," I concurred.

"But," he went on, ignoring me, "we have amassed quite a lot of new evidence or knowledge, and against incredible odds we have another person who is susceptible to this power."

"Am I? But nothing like Tim's experience has ever happened to me."

"Now are you sure?"

She nodded her head definitely. "Yes, positive. That is, except the two mental contactings, but that is different, isn't it?"

"Actually, it may all be part of the same thing." Professor Stewart got out of his chair and began to wander around the room in thought. Perhaps he needed his favourite desk chair to think this one through.

He didn't, however. What he'd done was to fall into the role of lecturer questioned by a student in a lecture. He normally paced the lecture room to find answers. Now he was pacing the lounge of the Black Swan.

"The human brain gives off all sorts of signals," he lectured us, but we weren't worried because we were very interested.

"Brain waves, we call them. Some of them we can detect with modern instruments."

"Go on, Professor," I prompted him.

"The most commonly known waves are beta waves which are given are given off by a normal attentive conscious person. Alpha waves are detected when one is in a state of meditation and restful awareness. Theta waves occur when you are nearly asleep, and delta waves are associated with deep sleep. These are waves we know about and can detect, but there is no doubt that the brain vibrates and hums with a multitude of brain waves. Just as our eyes are able to detect a continuous transmission of wavelengths in the visible spectrum, and our ears a continuous range in a different area of electro-magnetic spectrum of waves, one can hypothesise that the brain is able to receive and very likely transmit a continuous ethereal range of transmissions."

Kate was on the edge of her seat. "And you think that Tim and I have been receiving each other's signals?"

The professor nodded, still deep in thought. "Yes, I do."

"But why hasn't it happened before?" I asked the obvious question. He took off his glasses and stopped pacing in front of us.

"Just think. The universe began twenty billion years ago," he said in a reverent tone that commanded an appreciation of those endless years. "The Earth has been here for a mere fraction of that time and man a further fraction of the earth's millions of years. Of man's three million years, he has been civilised for just a few thousand years and it took him most of that time to find out where his brain is actually located. It is only in the past few decades that the bulk of his knowledge and awareness of his mental processes has been gathered." He paused. "Have I answered your question, Tim?"

"You mean that perhaps the human mind is reaching the point for a further leap forward and this inter-contact will provide the means?"

He nodded. "We know about you, Tim," he laid a hand on Kate's shoulder, "and now about you, Kate. Are there more? Are we about to see a landslide of awareness and interthought, which will take the human race a further step out of the animal mire?"

"Evolution," whispered Kate.

"Exactly that, Kate, but that's enough for tonight. . ." He peered at the carriage clock on the mantelpiece above the fire, forgetting that he had his glasses in one hand. "It's getting on for half past one and I'm not as young as I used to be. Let's continue our great thoughts tomorrow. I'm ready for bed."

I had to admit that my experience of the afternoon had tired me, and though stimulated by talk and world-shattering ideas, the suggestion of bed caused my eyelids to droop.

I suspect that we looked a pretty tired, shattered group as I gave my hand to Kate Bishop to help her unwind from the depths of her chair. She was very tall herself, I noticed, probably just a shade under six feet.

We all parted company on the first landing to disappear into our respective holes in the wall. I didn't take much notice of my bedroom and virtually fell into bed and, a few instants of time later, into a deep sleep. After the excitement of the day I wouldn't have been surprised to find that despite my tiredness I couldn't sleep. However, my fears were groundless and the next thing I knew was the awakening awareness that something was different. I became aware of the sound of cars driving past on the road, of voices and of bells. Yes, it was the bells which woke me on the Sunday morning. Well, a bell anyway. It was the church bell calling people to Sunday service.

I lay for a few minutes recollecting the events of the previous day and attempting to put some sense and logicality into them. That, I thought, might be a mistake. It might be because we apply logical thought progressing logically from one premise to the next that we had failed to penetrate into the inner mysteries of the brain. I came to the conclusion that I didn't know how not to think logically, and *that* might be my big mental block.

I put this profound thought to the professor when he appeared for breakfast as I was finishing off a plateful of bacon, egg, sausage and tomatoes.

"It could be a problem, I agree," he said as he perused the 'Good Morning Menu', "but that isn't Kate Bishop's problem, is it?"

"How do you know?"

He didn't answer that question until he'd placed his order.

"How do I know?" he asked. "*No* woman thinks in a logical way."

I laughed at his bias. "Surely, in this age of equality, you can't make a statement like that?"

"I do certainly. They may have sexual equality and equal wages, etc., and even some of them a smattering of logical thought, but at heart they think in a different way to us."

"Who do, Professor?" Kate had arrived unseen.

"You do." He was unabashed. Kate regarded him with an amused smile plucking at her lips. None of us looked a great deal different to the previous day, as we'd all checked in unexpectedly without a change of clothes. In fact I'd had to borrow an electric razor from Reception. Yet somehow Kate was different. Her heavy sweater and skirt still effectively hid the outlines of her just under six-foot figure, but in the light of day, with the morning sun reflecting off the glasses and mirrors in the breakfast room, she had a presence – that something which isn't beauty but which nevertheless turns heads.

"Don't take any notice of him, Kate. He's only an old biased professor." I pulled out a chair for her to sit down, which she did, conveying thanks without speaking.

"Oh, but I agree with him, Tim."

The professor guffawed at that. "You see, Tim, that is where you've been going wrong all these years. You looked on them as equals. They're not – they don't want equality, they *know* they are superior. Isn't that right, Kate?"

She acknowledged him with a graceful nod. "Yes, Professor, that is quite correct, but don't shatter Tim's illusions all at once."

For some minutes the delivery of their breakfasts interrupted the conversation. Now, suddenly, Kate changed from cheerful bantering and inconsequential chatter to a very serious tone.

"However, I concede that perhaps just at this moment we do need some logical thought. What is the next move, where do we go from here?"

The professor was busy bashing the top of an egg with a teaspoon.

"I take it, young lady, that things intrigue you enough for you to want to join our experiments?"

"Of course, how can I not now? I've been worried for weeks and now, this morning, I feel a new woman now that I know there is nothing to worry about."

"My dear," he covered her hand with his own large gnarled one, "that is being too presumptuous. Perhaps there is nothing to fear, but if you come into this thing I can promise you fear. The unknown always breeds fear."

"But I won't be on my own, will I? I'll have you two with me," she said gently. It seemed inconceivable that it was only yesterday that we had met. Yesterday evening at that, too, and already a mutual bond had been forged between the three of us.

"Okay" The professor was suddenly business-like again.

"We'd already taken the decision before we came across you last evening that we needed to confirm this link with historic religious sites."

"Can we do that today?" Kate was keen to get on.

"No, I would prefer not today." We waited while he crunched through half a slice of toast and marmalade.

"First of all, I have to be back in Sheffield by teatime today, and secondly before we put Tim into that position again I want him to do some training."

I was taken aback.

"Not the usual kind, Tim. I want you to train in meditation. Remember the monks of old. Let's see if in addition to confirming our experiment we can go a little further forward."

"I see what you mean, Professor. You think that if Tim trains in meditation the threshold of this access might be reduced and he could use it more easily."

"Yes, that's right. I know I was late for breakfast this morning, but I was awake quite early and I've been thinking." His toast lay forgotten now. "I'm convinced that the key to our inner mental processes is, in fact, a particular state of consciousness. When this self-induced, but critical, state of reverie is produced we can, if we know how, open up this vast store we've talked about."

"Right, Professor, I'll do that. But where? Some places are more conducive to that kind of thought than others. My cottage wouldn't be the right place, I'm sure."

"Tim, are you a practising Christian? Do you go to church?"

"Well, yes, I'm a Catholic actually." Now wasn't the time to go into a long discussion on religion and all the reservations and conditions which I personally put on formal religion and the reasons for acknowledging membership of any particular branch.

"Oh, I'm surprised," Kate exclaimed.

"Pardon, why?" She coloured – rather attractively, I thought.

"I don't know why I said that, Tim, but I didn't for some reason expect that you could be a Catholic."

The professor was observing us curiously and I wondered if he thought of us as specimens on a microscope slide to be carefully observed.

"Most Catholic churches are relatively recent buildings. Have you any objection to going into an Anglican Church?"

"No, why?"

"Well, if it had been warmer and lighter on an evening I would have recommended that you did your meditation on one of the old abbey sites. But it is obviously too cold for that."

"Sorry, I should have picked the summer for this operation."

"No, it's better now. There are fewer people around. Fewer people to disturb us. Is there an old parish church in Northallerton?"

Kate answered that without hesitation. "Yes, a very old one, and rather beautiful too. I'm an Anglican," she added needlessly.

"Right. Before next Saturday, Tim, get yourself into the church each night and practise for an hour, and next Saturday we'll meet again."

"Where this time?" asked Kate. "I'll join you again, Tim, but by arrangement this time."

"It's to be another abbey, you said, Professor?"

"Yes, well an abbey or a priory – I don't think it matters too much."

"There's Byland and Guisborough." I tried to think of more.

"Whitby... Rosedale," added Kate.

"Of course." I snapped my fingers. "I always forget about it because I go past it every day to work. Mount Grace Priory at Osmotherly. It's the ideal place if you think about it. It was built by the Carthusians who were, if I remember rightly, more like hermits than monks. They lived not only completely apart from the world, but also from each other."

"In order to meditate on their inner minds," mused the professor. "Yes, I think that will be just the place to go to next. Where shall we meet?"

"What about at the gate of Northallerton Parish Church?" I proposed.

"Yes, very appropriate," he acknowledged. "And you, Kate, can you make it for say twelve noon, next Saturday?"

"Just try to keep me away."

And so our weekend finally evaporated into the air in Helmsley market place as, having paid our respective bills, we each sought our cars.

The professor was first to leave, followed not too long after by a white Ford Escort.

I kept the Escort in sight on the way back across the moors towards Thirsk. I followed it carefully down Sutton Bank and through the village of the Whitestonecliffe. We both followed the road into Thirsk's market place and took the Northallerton road out again.

It was with some reluctance that I let it carry on alone when I turned off at my village road and followed the road down the bank into the village proper. My cottage was near the west end, along past the church and the pub. Although I'd lived there on my own for some months now, for the first time it felt cold and lonely as I closed the door behind me.

Chapter Eight
Meditation

I did go to church that Sunday, but it was to the Catholic church in Thirsk where I usually went each Sunday. I must admit that I wasn't too conscious of the Mass and the responses. Although, I suppose I managed to stand, kneel and sit in the correct places, I never consciously took part in the formal prayers. But then the mass is one form of prayer and perhaps I was taking part in another form. I was attempting to meditate, but the professor seemed to be right and I never achieved a peaceful mind. On the other hand, perhaps that had nothing to do with the church. It may be that my mind was so active with thoughts of the weekend, that it was just impossible that evening to achieve a calm, tranquil, peaceful level of the mind.

On the Monday morning, however, I was able to forget about the weekend completely. For some reason Bob Atwell was away and I was thoroughly engrossed in the transfer of a dual computer system from our office block, where it had been on test for some six months, to the new process plant, where it would eventually control the production of another chemical deemed to be necessary by our technological society. In consequence, it was getting on for seven o'clock before I arrived in Northallerton on my way home from work and instituted the first part of the professor's request. I parked alongside the church wall behind the church and walked via the little pedestrian gate in the back wall to the church porch.

Only then did it occur to me that the church could be locked, but there did seem to be a low level of light behind the stained glass windows. I tried the handle and the door opened quietly and easily, and I was able to step inside. I'd many times walked and driven past the church with its clock tower, but I'd never before been inside. I walked across the stone flagged floor to face up the centre aisle. It was, in the half light cast by four electric light bulbs, rather beautiful with its ancient stonework and pillars climbing into the dark recesses of the roof. There was no other person in the church, but I still tried to tread softly as I walked up the centre aisle.

Yes, the professor was right. This place had atmosphere. It could be felt as I paused at a pew and, pulling a kneeler, I knelt down. It exuded from the sandstone walls and it rained down on me from the timbers in the darkest reaches of the roof. The walls around, in common with many old churches carried memorials and statues of people long dead. The stone floor was made up of memorial slabs too, perhaps even gravestones. The entire architecture of the place produced a marvellous symphony of *atmosphere*.

As I knelt in the dimly-lit church, I felt like a conductor banging his baton for attention preparatory to conducting this orchestra of atmospheres. I was going to try to put it into some sort of order and see if it in its turn could do something for me. For some minutes I concentrated on clearing out my mind, or at least that part of it that I dealt with every day. I closed my eyes and waited.

Although I thought that I was reasonably successful at holding rational thoughts at bay, nothing happened except that the darkness in front of my closed eyes whirled with little red and blue dots of colour, whirling in a whirlpool of darkness and light. There was nothing unusual in that, though, it was only an effect produced by the eyes receptors, often achieved at night in bed. It was bitterly cold outside with a frost already forming on the paving stones in the square, but the church seemed to be quite warm and it radiated spiritual warmth and friendliness. I opened my eyes and picked out the altar indirectly illuminated through the tall thin windows by the sodium street lights outside, and instead of holding thoughts in check I allowed them to wander at random. But again, perhaps, I was too tired, for random thoughts didn't come. I closed my eyes again and watched the red dots disappearing into the central invisible vortex to be inexplicably replaced by new ones willing to follow the same random path to destruction.

I pressed my eyelids and the red and blue dots disappeared becoming large blobs of interacting yellow. I slightly released the pressure and a light pool of sky blue appeared. The next pattern change was produced because a stray noise of the church door being opened caused me unconsciously to remove my hands from my eyes.

The whirlpool didn't return. This time it was lines of colour making up a strange foaming seashore of impressions. I was for a time unaware of the person who had entered the church. I wasn't bothered whether it was the vicar or the curate, or someone else seeking their own peace from the modern world outside. I was intent on my meditation. Whoever had come in was still behind me however, for no one came up the aisle or passed by on either of the two outside aisles.

The colours had now ceased and the blackness was absolute. I had only to open my eyes of course to re-establish contact with the world but my eyes were sealed with will-power. Almost, I had a feeling of panic that I couldn't open my eyes at all, but my other senses detected reassurance around me. From across time an awareness was being superimposed on my mind and it only needed that blackness to lift and I would know. But the blackness didn't lift. It shimmered a little around the edges. It turned a shade of light lighter from time to time and it grew thinner so that I could almost convince myself that I could see those vast banks of— Suddenly the all pervading peace was shattered by noise. The noise rocked back and forth across my dark screen of meditation, making it form again and radiating electromagnetic waves of repulsing sound. The attempt was shattered as my cloud of darkness broke up into shooting stars which forced my eyes open and broke my reverie.

The world had broken in again with the sounding of the church clock. It was striking eight o'clock and my hour had fled. For a moment I sat back onto the seat and allowed my everyday senses to find themselves again and establish normal contact with each other. When I felt my sense of balance restored, I left the pew and walked a little unsteadily towards the rear of the church. As I approached the dimly-lit back, I sensed another person in the rear pew who was observing me. She seemed to be all coat and hood – obviously intent on keeping the cold at bay.

"Hello, Tim, don't you recognise me?"

In my current state of mind the whisper seemed to come not from the figure but from the air. I stopped dead by the back seat as she, for it was obviously a she, threw back her hood. But she didn't need to do that for I did indeed recognise the voice. It was as unexpected as it was welcome. I hadn't expected to see her again until the following Saturday.

"Kate!" I exclaimed. "What are you doing here?"

"Well, I thought I would come and practise meditation with you."

"But how did you know when I'd be here?" I looked needlessly at my watch. "It's eight o'clock."

"To tell you the truth, I didn't," she admitted. "But you had promised the professor that you would come here each evening and so since five o'clock I've popped in three times looking for you, and the fourth time I was lucky."

I moved into the pew with her. "And so tell me, Tim, have you managed anything tonight? I've been trying ever so hard for the last half hour to make our minds meet, but I couldn't feel yours." She looked hopefully at me, but though I wished that I could have said yes, I couldn't. So instead I stood up and shook my head.

"No, nothing. Come on, it's too cold to talk in here, let's find a warm pub. We could both probably do with a drink." Without waiting for a reply which might have been a yes or a no, I led the way out of the church.

"Where's your car?" I asked, pausing in the church porch uncertain of which way to turn.

"Actually I haven't got it here, I walked."

"Oh." I suddenly realised that I didn't know where she lived.

"My car is this way," I said, pointing. "We may as well drive around in it to the main street." It was on the short drive around to the Black Bull that I extracted the information that Kate lived in a flat on South Parade. She kept her gloves on so that I couldn't even secretly see if she was engaged. But I wasn't too bothered about that tonight or even about the possibility that she mightn't like to be seen with a man in a High Street pub. Okay, I had rather pulled her along with me instead of asking if she would like to go, but on the other hand she hadn't said no and she was tagging along with me.

After the freezing air outside, the pub, though virtually deserted, was lovely and warm and, in common with lots of places in this part of the world, had a nice log fire crackling in a basket grate. I sorted the drinks out at the bar – a whisky and dry ginger for me and a snowball for Kate. I paid for the drinks and carried them across to the fireplace, where she had pulled up a couple of chairs. It wasn't long before the heat of the fire had penetrated and we were beginning to feel a little warm and I took off my anorak. Kate followed suit and took off her coat. Mine wasn't the only head to turn as she reached for her drink. There were no heavy all-enveloping sweaters and skirts tonight. No, tonight Kate Bishop was dressed in an up-to-the-minute figure-hugging thin woollen cream dress. It matched her light complexion and golden hair perfectly. High heeled boots, making her virtually as tall as me, and the high neckline were very appropriate to the weather outside. This time I could see her hands and they were completely bare of rings.

"This is certainly warmer than in the church, Tim." She sat back into the chair again, erect and proud.

"It certainly is. How long were you there, Kate?"

"Oh, I would think about half an hour."

I was surprised.

"As long that? Actually, now I come to think about it I don't seem to have been there for an hour." I paused and took a long drink.

"Why did you come tonight, Kate?" The flickering firelight seemed to hold her eyes.

"I believe the professor, Tim. I think we are on the verge of an evolutionary breakthrough, and as I seem to be, in a little way, part of it, I want to help as much as possible. That means that besides your efforts to break through, *I* have to try as well. My experiences haven't been the same as yours, but perhaps in a way they are. We must tackle this from as many directions as we can at once. You are the only other person I know with this. . ." She looked for a word to describe it and failed, but her eyes sought mine and held them without thinking.

"Tim, if we work closely together on this we might both come out at the other side. Singly we might achieve little, or we might not survive."

I must admit that I had not thought about that angle before. I had never even contemplated that any ill could befall me as a result of those experiments. Suddenly, a little shiver formed at the base of my spine, gathered strength and burst its way outwards and up my backbone. It erupted into a final shudder which made my shoulders jolt. Kate saw it but didn't comment and neither did I. It was too late for second thoughts: we would both have to live with our own fears and shivers from now on. It was a question of whether we would bear them alone or together.

Kate was still holding my eyes with hers.

"Tim. I want to come with you each evening to Northallerton Church, and also each time that you attempt to break into this thing I want to be there. You must promise me never to attempt it on your own."

I was aware that her hands had made contact with mine. They were long and soft. I could feel her tension being transmitted into my hand. Her hands gripped mine tightly and I could feel a slight tremor. Inexplicably I knew that she had no commitment to anyone else and I was glad. I gripped her hands even tighter with my own. I wanted to say many things to Kate Bishop, but I had only known her for a few days. Instead all I said was, "Yes, Kate, I promise."

And so quietly, if emotionally, our pact was sealed. For some minutes we sat tightly clasping our hands and looking into each other's eyes, each trying to read a future in the other's grey depths, but it was impossible to see. The door opening to let in another party of people broke our little self-induced spell and we both sat back in our respective chairs.

After some minutes, during which neither of us felt the need for speech, Kate took what was at first sight a completely different track.

"Do you believe in God, Tim?"

I had a feeling that I knew what she was getting at, but nevertheless I gave the cautious conventional answer.

"Well, I do profess to be a Catholic."

She nodded. "And I am Anglican, but I ask again. Do you believe in God?"

Once again I avoided a direct answer. "Do you mean the conventional God of Christianity?"

She never asked again, but merely raised her eyebrows waiting for my answer. It may have been my meditation period in Northallerton Church or my recent visits to the ancient centres of religion, but I was able to answer her more clearly and certainly than I would at any time in the last few years.

"Yes."

"Yes, I do too, but *what* is God, Tim?"

I took a deep breath before plunging on.

"Well, Kate, I'm sure that God is nothing like any of us imagines. I've looked up the meaning of the word from time to time and the definition is the Sole Supreme Being. I really believe that that is as near as anyone on this earth will get to describing God."

She now had a little frown.

"But that isn't the Catholic view or for that matter other Christians' views either, is it? They go much further building up a whole theology."

"No," I acknowledged. "It isn't official party doctrine and I suppose I wouldn't be acknowledged as a Catholic if I were to spread this as a sole doctrine."

"But then why are you a Catholic?"

"That, my dear Kate, is a good question. It's one I've asked myself time and time over the years. Why am I a Catholic, or to be more precise why do I go to a Catholic church?" I paused for a moment collecting my scattered thoughts.

"It's the first time I've had to say exactly why to another person, and I think the answer is simple. I could philosophise at length, but the true answer is probably – from habit. You see, I was given a formal Catholic education at a school run by priests and I know most of the dogma and formal institutional answers. It wasn't until I went to university, and met the world head on, that among all the other questions I asked, I asked what is all this dogma? What does it all mean?" For the first time in my life I was opening my soul to another person and that mutual contact was heightened as I felt Kate's hand creep into my arm again.

"I went to discussion groups and talked about them with the university Chaplain, but I never arrived at any answers that satisfied me. In all that time I continued going to church from habit. I often wondered why I was there at all, because I didn't believe any of it. I'd lost faith. I continued in the same mental turmoil when I left university and went to work. I even reached the stage where I didn't believe in the existence of God at all, but that strong training from my school days continued to reach out through the years and held on to me. At times the hold was tenuous, but yet just strong enough to push me most Sundays into the nine or ten-thirty mass. I was not allowed to forget the question. Your question, Kate. Is there a God?" Her hand tightened on my arm. "If I'd stopped going to church, perhaps I'd have forgotten there was a question, but every week without fail the question had me again and again. I listened to sermons – rubbishy sermons, good sermons, wishy-washy sermons, sermons breathing fire and brimstone. I ignored some sermons, and after the second Vatican Council I often felt like standing up in church and saying what a load of claptrap the priest was talking. But, Kate, slowly and imperceptibly, I moved into quieter, calmer waters. I didn't have the answers. Many people think they have the answers, but they haven't really. They only have the questions. My peace of mind came when I came to the realisation that there *are* questions, but that the answers are in all probability intellectually beyond the human race." I had got myself into full flow and Kate was making no attempt to break in. She continued to listen attentively

"To live in this world, you don't have to have the answers, but the human race, being what it is, tries to produce the answers – hence the great religious faiths of the world grew up. Each in its own way believed in God. It took the one central theme and then built scaffolding around that central theme. Over the years the scaffolding became more massive and all-encompassing. Some of it was strong, built with foundations, but some of it was weak, and other parts were put in to prop up the weaker struts. From time to time over the centuries the whole lot crumbled away and collapsed, usually when human development reached a particular point of advancement and realisation of the physical world and laws. These structures were built and rebuilt by men who then went on to defend their particular structure against those who sought to pull it down, and hence we've had many religious wars largely because of the uncompromising nature of man. He sets up stated positions and sticks to them, and in fighting for them they become positions more positively held than ever. If you've fought and died for an ideal, it must be right." I paused for a moment and emptied my glass. The firelight was holding a fascination for Kate again, but then unexpectedly she took up my theme.

"You mean that we in our own little sects of the Christian faith tend to hang on to them because of the sacrifices made by our forefathers?"

I nodded. "Yes, you see, what if they weren't right, what if they were wrong? Just think of what we know of pagan religions and their sacrifices to the gods – in particular the Sun god. To those people, at their stage of development, the Sun must have been that sole supreme being. It gave them life and light and heat and food. His priests mistakenly interpreted his need for sacrifices."

"And we know they were wrong, Tim, and so you ask are we wrong too?"

"Yes, Kate, I ask that and I believe that too. We are wrong because we are at one particular stage in the evolution of man. We can only understand and assimilate so much information. That so much is in fact quite a lot, so our scaffolding and professed beliefs are complicated. But how do we compare to man ten thousand years hence? In ten thousand years our efforts will seem small compared with the world as it will be then."

"You mean if it lasts until then?" That particular question halted me in my tracks.

"Do you doubt it?"

"Don't you, Tim?"

"Give me your glass, Kate, and I'll get you another drink before I answer that one."

I refilled our glasses at the bar before returning to the fireside. My chair was already close to Kate's so my attempt to pull it closer came to nothing.

"You were going to answer me, Tim," Kate asked as soon as I settled down and retrieved her hand into mine.

"No, I don't doubt it, Kate. Whatever happens, man, or evolved man," I carefully amended "...will last for many years yet. What you might ask, Kate, is, will Christianity last that long?"

She nodded and obliged me with the rhetorical question, "Will it?"

"That is another question. Perhaps an evolved form of Christianity will be in existence, but it will be totally different from our beliefs today. That brings me back to your question why do I go to a Catholic church? The answer is that it is simply the set of scaffolding that I know well and that I'm most familiar with. My one central truth is that God exists – in what form I don't know, but my scaffolding helps me think about God. It keeps the idea alive in men's minds. From time to time it deals with God wrongly, but that is human nature. Why did you ask if I believed in God, Kate?"

"I'm not sorry I did, you know, Tim. It opened a floodgate in you, didn't it? But your answer certainly gave me something to think about."

"But," I insisted, "*why* did you ask the question?"

"I asked because for the first time in my life *I*'ve been forced to ask that question. If you, or you and I, or all of us are on the brink of some tremendous mental evolutionary breakthrough, it will turn the world in which we live upside down. You might have questioned the existence of God for years, Tim, but not I. I've been brought up unquestioningly as an Anglican, sure and certain in my faith and knowledge of God. Now I realise that that was a childlike-acceptance and I'm glad that I was able to ask you the question at the point in time my doubt arose. I've obviously got to think it through for myself, but your road is at least marked out for me and I may not have so much heartache about it as you've had."

We both ignored the self-evident fact that it was also me that had caused her to question the main point of her faith.

"It's rather sad, isn't it, that over all these years, even in the time of Christianity, men have fought and died over the interpretation of God and religion. If you are right, Tim, it hardly matters whether the transubstantiation interpretation of Communion is correct or whether it is consubstantive."

"That's true. Kate, in fact it's almost certain that neither interpretation is correct or any other interpretation that the human mind can put on it."

"You were very careful then to say – almost certain. . ."

"Yes, on my philosophy, if I were to exclude the possibility that either of these interpretations was in fact correct, then I myself would be falling into the age-old trap of being dogmatic. So I say that either could be true, and it doesn't matter a great deal if some people hold one idea and others the other or indeed any other idea."

"And if you were to have children, Tim, would you bring them up as Catholics?" I took the question at its simple face value with no thought as to future possibilities.

"That would depend on whether my wife was a Catholic or not. If she was an Anglican for example, with a strong personal faith which would give my children some idea of a God which they would take with them into their future, I wouldn't mind that. But, paradoxically, after all I've said, I do believe that if they aren't propped up with one form of scaffold or another, then they have nothing, not even an imperfect grasp on God. They do need a structure to hang on to. As long as they are aware of all its failings and whichever one they chose, I would hope that as they grow up I would be able to influence them and perhaps give them my own thoughts and prevent them becoming entrenched in one idea or another."

We had finished our drinks while we had talked and the fire had gradually burnt itself out and was now dropping its last embers into the ash tray below. We seemed to spend our time these days staring into fires and thinking great thoughts, straining to extend the area of human thought.

"Tim, I want to go home. It's ten o'clock. I need to do a lot of thinking. Will you walk home with me?" I ignored the fact that I had a car outside. Wherever our mental paths might take us I was very happy to be walking home with this golden-haired Greek goddess beside me.

We said goodbye to the landlord and, pulling our hoods up against the cold, ventured forth onto the High Street. The night was sharp and clear and it didn't take us long to walk the length of the High Street onto South Parade. I stopped as we turned the corner opposite the library and looked up at the sky. As with many cold clear nights the sky was cloudless and shone with its billions of pinpricks of light.

"Look up, Kate, if you want to know which single thing held me to a belief in a God – whatever he may be. Look at the order up there – planets, suns, stars, galaxies, universes, and so on. What holds them in order? Where did they come from? Against that immensity, man is nothing – an infinitesimal speck of dust in the cosmos. What gives him the right to pontificate and fight over what God is? God created all that. He is what he is, regardless of what man thinks he is."

Chapter Nine
Communication

The next evening I drove into the grammar school car park and went into the main entrance of the school. Before parting the previous evening, I had agreed to pick Kate up from the school on my way to Northallerton Church, and that was the reason I was investigating the interior of a school for the first time since I had left my own Teesside school. It was six o'clock before I reached the school and it looked pretty deserted, but investigation of the front corridor revealed a staff room about halfway along and I found Kate amidst several piles of English exercise books.

As I knocked and opened the door and peered around the screen, I caught the quick flash of pleasure which passed across her face, before she assumed the formal 'school ma'am' image.

"Hello, Kate, are you ready for church?"

"Yes, Tim."

She gathered her books together into a large bag, and with no further conversation tucked her hand under my arm as I took her bag. We were outside again before the silence was broken again by me.

"I hope you don't want to walk tonight."

"No, I'm quite happy for you to drive me today."

It had snowed earlier in the day, but it was now turning to a horrible slush, which made walking not only unpleasant but very difficult. In fact, all in all, it wasn't quite the sort of night for sitting or kneeling in a cold church for an hour.

We let ourselves into the church, which was in fact quite a lot warmer than outside. As with the previous night it was only half lit. This time we knelt side by side for the prescribed hour of meditation. We struggled for calm and peace and that something, but it eluded us – certainly for that Tuesday evening.

On the next day I found out where Bob Atwell was. He'd been called out early on the Monday morning to solve a major mechanical problem on our construction site. It was, he told me on the telephone, unlikely that he would be able to get into Billingham during the week and he was most frustrated that he was unable to have a long chat about events after he'd left Helmsley on the Saturday. He was pleased to know that the next meeting was scheduled for Saturday and he promised to meet us at Mount Grace Priory.

"In fact," he mused, "why don't you come round to our house on Friday evening for dinner? You can bring me right up to date."

"Well, it could be a little awkward. You see. . ." and I told him how I was being joined every evening by Kate at the church, ". . .and I could hardly leave her, could I?"

"Oh, oh, it's like that, is it? Already. . ." I could hear him chortling away to himself on the other end.

"That's no problem, Tim. You know you'll both be welcome, and Margaret will be pleased to see this blonde I've been telling her about, that I nearly had to chase all round the North East."

Se we left it at that until Friday, and I filled in the rest of the week by working hard during the day and meditating hard during the evening. By Friday it had become something of a ritual to drive into the school, pick up Kate, and drive down to church. Rituals do tend to become familiar, and as with the rituals of religion, perhaps they have the purpose of lulling us into a particular frame of mind. As with previous evenings, we knelt in the main body of the church about halfway down on the right-hand side. There was only a small difference. As far as I could see, there were two candles lit on the main altar for some reason, and one of the electric lights previously alight was not on. I concentrated on the flickering flame of one of the candles and again willed my workday mind to peace. Practice was certainly proving to make things easier. I attained a level of peace in about ten minutes, but the curtain of darkness stubbornly refused to lift. I was willing it to move. I wanted again to see all the stored knowledge which I had glimpsed so tantalisingly last Saturday.

The flame alternately leapt and guttered on the altar as the draughts in the old building attacked it. The flame leapt up, a golden crown around the wick, a golden speck of light in the darkness, gold like Kate's hair, and suddenly, framed in the apparently enlarged flame, I could see Kate's face and she was talking to me – but I couldn't quite hear.

I shook my head. I was supposed to be meditating, not going to sleep and dreaming. Kate was beside me, but I looked at the flame again. No, her face wasn't *in* the flame. It was sort of superimposed in the air in front of the flame and she was trying to communicate. I meditated on this ethereal figure for some minutes before I had the presence of mind to look at Kate and I experienced a most peculiar sensation. With my eyes I could see her face as it really was – long and white, framed in her long golden hair, at peace, with her eyes closed, showing off her long fair eyelashes. Sort of superimposed on her was the ethereal image, eyes open and smiling, speaking, reaching out to me, but still I couldn't quite hear.

The big latch on the door at the back of the church cracked loudly into the silence and echoed around, jumping in and out of the nooks and crannies. It was the curate coming in to. . . to do I don't know what, but the noise made Kate's real eyes flicker again. For an instant of time her eyes were empty of life, and then it flooded in and the ethereal image wavered and was gone. I glanced back to the candles, but they only flickered on, wildly fighting the new onslaught being launched from the open church door.

We ignored the incomer. I could tell by looking at her face that Kate had felt something strange too.

"What is it, Kate?" I whispered.

"Don't you know, Tim?" she asked.

"Tell me."

"I contacted your mind, Tim." Her eyes bored into mine. "'Couldn't you feel it?"

I shook my head. "No, but that explains what I thought was an apparition." I explained to her about her face.

"Tim, I can't explain how, but I was sort of turned to your thoughts, almost as though I could hear you thinking."

"Everything?"

"No, I don't think so. I think it was only what you wanted me to know." She smiled secretly to herself.

I looked at my watch. "Come on, we'll talk about it in the car or we'll be late for dinner at Bob's. We've got to get to Hartlepool, you know."

We retreated down the aisle and nodded good evening to the curate, who was looking curiously at us. We went quickly across the churchyard into the car before we spoke again, and it wasn't until we'd called at Kate's flat and raced around to tidy up before setting out for Bob's that we had time to recall the events in the church.

We headed out of Northallerton on the road leading to Clack Lane Ends where it joined the A19 North. Fortunately, the cold of the last few days had eased a little, as the road over Winton Bank could be quite treacherous with snow or ice around.

As we left the last street light of Northallerton behind, I happened to glance at Kate and she had a self-satisfied little smile on her lips.

"Kate, share it with me. What are you smiling at?" I'd caught her on the hop, for she started a little before she answered.

"I'm not sure that I should tell you."

That made me worried that she'd found out something during her brief encounter with my mind. I thought about the implications of non-permitted access to one's mind for some minutes. My silence obviously worried her in turn and she obviously decided to give a little more information.

"Tim, I didn't receive any more information than you were prepared to give out."

"Which was?"

"Well, put it like this, Timothy Drummond – *I love you* too."

Now that was the last thing I'd expected. But it was undeniably true. I'd known this girl less than a week, but I was head over heels in love with her. Quite remarkable for a man who'd steered a cautious course through the minefield all these years. I could only put it down to our meeting of minds as well as bodies, but now I was worried again. She'd contacted me, not me her, except that the vision had obviously been real in terms of the mind, brought about by her attempt at communication.

The distance and time taken to get to Hartlepool was shared with a comfortable silence while we both considered our new but declared positions. I'd taken a turn at the crossroads sure enough, but this was the least expected of all possible results.

*

We arrived at Bob Atwell's at about half past eight and were warmly welcomed by a red-faced Bob. He always seemed to develop a red face when he was happy and tonight he was happy. We were ushered into the lounge and introduced to a glass of sherry each.

"Margaret will be through in a few minutes. She's wrestling with the oven at the moment," he explained.

"Sit down." He indicated the chairs. There was no roaring fire tonight, but it was still nice and warm from Bob's underfloor heating system. It was the sort of house where it would have been nice to wander around in one's bare feet if that had been polite. In actual fact Bob was the sort of person who wouldn't have minded in the least if you did take you shoes off.

"Look," he explained, "if you don't mind, I'd prefer that we waited for Margaret before you tell me about what's happened. She's absolutely consumed with curiosity, so I'm sure you'll understand." He was juddering his right knee slightly, a sure sign that though he was confident enough, he was slightly embarrassed at asking to include his wife in the discussions.

"Yes, okay, Bob. Tell us: what's been the problem on the job this week to keep you away from the office?"

And that launched him off into a long technical discourse on the inadequacies of package plants, particularly when ordered via a main contractor. I very much doubt if Kate understood much of what was being said, but it filled the time until Margaret appeared and was introduced to Kate. I had met her a few times previously, not many, and she always seemed a very nice, quite inoffensive woman. She was smaller than Bob, but that didn't mean that he dominated her at all. In fact, a quick word from Margaret was enough to stop Bob in full flood, even with one of his boisterous risqué-type jokes, which he produced off a conveyor belt when he'd had a few drinks.

Introductions over, Margaret wanted us to sit down to dinner straight away before it spoiled, so we moved to the dining-room and joined in the work of dividing up the food between four people. It was Bob, unable to contain his curiosity any longer, who finally asked:

"Come on then, Tim. Story time. I've told Margaret what happened up to me leaving the Black Swan, Helmsley, last Saturday. It's episode two time now, and you're the reader."

And so I related what had occurred and what we'd talked about and speculated on before we left Helmsley. With very few interruptions for re-explanations I reached the events of earlier this evening, and left them astounded with the apparent explanation that Kate was able to communicate directly with my mind.

Bob returned to his potato croquettes, which he'd stopped attacking as I'd described the scene in Northallerton Church, and pointed his loaded fork at me.

"You realise what this means, don't you?"

"It could mean an awful lot of things, Bob."

"Yes, but one thing is that there are two minds involved in this thing. Yours seems to be particularly sensitive to particular geographical locations and the effect is to enlarge your known stored knowledge. But Kate's is different. She hasn't experienced this apparent enlargement of knowledge, but she has the ability to communicate which you appear not to have."

"Do you mean to imply that they are two different gifts?" I used the word for want of a more explanatory one.

"It could be, Tim, or..." - he munched his pork fillet thoughtfully - "...it could be the same gift which each of you is using in a different way and which with practice you could both expand into each other's."

"I'm not sure I want to expand my facility to do what Tim is doing." Kate gave a little shudder, but Bob wouldn't accept that.

"But, Kate, don't you think if you have this gift that you have to expand it and develop it for the good of humanity?"

Kate turned her grey eyes on Bob. She was genuinely concerned at his question and didn't treat it in the apparently flip way he'd asked it.

"If I was truly convinced that it was for the good of humanity, yes, I would develop it. But is it? That's the question I can't answer."

Margaret had said very little up to now, but she had an unsuspected depth to her.

"Kate, my dear," she interposed, softly and unexpectedly into the discussion, "I think that no matter how much you worry at that question you'll never know an answer to it. I don't think it's up to you to decide whether you will or whether you won't. You *have* to develop it. If, as you've all postulated..." - she encompassed us all with her knife - "...this is an evolutionary step, *you* cannot decide not to take it. You are only one person in the world. You may advance or retard evolution, but you won't stop it."

Bob was nodding in agreement with his wife, although he was looking a little surprised at her.

"You see, Tim, she's not just a pretty face." She accepted the implied compliment with the trace of a smile, but carried on, almost ignoring his interruption.

"Look around us in the world today. It's all in a vast turmoil. The standards of the past are collapsing. Everyone is casting around, looking for something else to hold onto. The age of technology has thrown many cultures into one melting pot. As yet nothing has come out of the pot. It's like when two vast rivers meet. At the point of meeting there is immense confusion and violence, but slowly the turbulence dies down and the rivers merge safely and carry on as one new great river. So with the present turmoils a new different culture will emerge. That is what we are talking about, the forging of the next leap in evolution. From where we sit tonight we think that it could be the advancement of our minds through a more enlightened individual, and hopefully a group, consciousness. No, Kate, the decision is not yours to take."

Margaret scraped the rest of her gravy onto her last piece of pork, while we all recovered in the silence from the impact of her words. Unusually lengthy for Margaret, there was no trite reply to be made, not even from Bob. It was Kate who finally spoke into the spreading ripple of shock waves.

"You are right, of course, Margaret," and so she was. We all agreed that she was right, but it was nevertheless an uncomfortable thought.

"We haven't thought this evolutionary thing through properly, you know, have we?" Bob asked of no one in particular.

"What does it mean or what will it mean? If you think about it, there are all sorts of possibilities, aren't there? Just take this communication business. If there are all these ethereal wave bands around which we can tap into when we can manipulate our brains better, perhaps we will be able to communicate with other things."

"You mean like animals?" I asked him.

"Yes, that sort of thing, or maybe plants and trees. They are alive, aren't they? I know it's a different sort of life, but whose to say that they aren't projecting knowledge into this vast communications network we are hypothesising?"

"Yes," mused Kate. "We could go on and on on that track, couldn't we? What about communicating with rocks and the earth?"

"But," protested, Bob, "rock is dead. At least we know that trees and plants are alive and growing."

"And how can you be so sure that rock is dead?" I asked him. "Don't forget the geological timespans are millions of years. Perhaps they are living too, but in a completely different timescale to us. To them they are living on a universe timescale. Communications have to be over millions of years and across vast reaches of space. In fact, perhaps as yet they, if they *are* alive, haven't even noticed man's presence. We know that everything is composed of some sort of molecular structure, even man. So perhaps inherent in that is built in communications. Our problem then is to find the link and interface to it via our brains."

Bob shrugged his shoulders, "Yes, okay. I accept that as well."

"Have you thought about the implications of all this new knowledge on teaching," the teacher asked. "How are we going to be able to deal with all the amount of information in a normal way?"

"What is the normal way, Kate? You and Margaret and Tim there are used to the teaching done in schools. If what we are talking about was to evolve, then teaching would have to evolve too. Instead of teaching facts, which is how we do it now, we would have to teach guidelines to people for how to find and deal with facts as and when they are wanted for specialist activities. It would be a much more fluid and ill-defined task."

"Thank you very much, Bob. I'm not sure that I would still want to be a teacher in your new world."

"Oh, it's just because you're not used to it. After this evolutionary step what you do now, Kate, will probably seem very childish and simple. Shall we go through to the lounge if we've all finished?"

Somehow the meal had been consumed. We'd discussed our new communications world back and forth across the table and the food had disappeared without our being aware of eating. It was a pity really because I'm sure that Margaret had spent much time and effort on it, and it had certainly looked nice when she had brought it in. But our subject matter was all engrossing and it continued to hold us while we had coffee.

After pouring the coffee, Margaret went to a bookshelf and after searching for a few minutes pulled out a book and found a page.

"I thought I'd seen something that was very appropriate to what we've been talking about. Listen..." – she drew a deep breath and read – "...'The human brain is an enchanted loom where millions of flashing shuttles weave a dissolving pattern, always meaningful, never abiding. It is as if the Milky Way entered as a cosmic dance...' That was written by a man called Sir Charles Sherrington. Do you think he had ideas like we've had?"

"Now that's an interesting question, Margaret," I answered her. "How many other people have experienced these feelings, these evolutionary thoughts we might almost call them. Have they happened before? If so, did they fail to evolve or did they back off? We might not succeed, I suppose."

"No, Tim, *you* might not succeed," agreed Margaret, "but that doesn't have to deter you. Someone, somewhere will succeed if there is an evolutionary path there, and it might be you and Kate. It really might be."

Chapter Ten
A Further Advance Via Mount Grace

My shaving ritual was about halfway through when the telephone shrilled. I contemplated ignoring it. After all, if I'd got up earlier, I would have been out by now and I couldn't have answered it. Isn't it strange how a telephone insists on being answered. It rudely interrupts conversations, meetings, dinners, and shaves, and always gets away with it.

"Hello," I grunted, giving my telephone number. I had been up until about two o'clock in the morning as it had been well after midnight before we got away from Bob Atwell's the previous evening.

"Hello, Tim, Frank Cooper here." We ploughed on through the usual inconsequential conversational results of making and answering a telephone call until a mutually acceptable point was reached when the purpose of the call could be revealed.

"Tim – Eileen and Gillian are away this weekend at her mother's. I thought I'd have a drive down to Northallerton and stay over the night, if it's okay by you?"

"That would be fine' Frank, except—"

"If it's inconvenient, just say so."

"I would, don't worry, but I've arranged to go to Mount Grace Priory today," and then I went on to give him an abridged edition description of everything that had happened since our day out to Housesteads.

". . .but please come anyway. You can come with us. You never know, you could be useful."

"Well, thank you very much," he commented, a little sarcastically.

"But," he added hastily before I simulated offence, "I would really like to get involved in this. It sounds pretty exciting stuff, the frontiers of science and all that."

I explained that we were meeting outside Northallerton Church at twelve noon. I glanced at my watch. It was already ten o'clock.

"Oh, I rather think in that case that I'll see you there at Mount Grace a bit later. I know it's only an hour and a half from here to Northallerton, but I've one or two things to sort out before I can leave."

"Well, I would think that we'll probably have lunch before we set off for Mount Grace anyway, getting there about one-ish."

"Okay, Tim, see you there then."

Now I could have got to Newcastle in time if the positions had been reversed, but Frank, I knew from experience, was not capable of being hurried. He would plough steadily through his preparations for going out. He would not deviate from his regular plan, and if that meant that he would be late, well then, he would be late.

I went back to the bathroom to finish off my interrupted shaving. Afterwards I had some toast for breakfast while trying to hold my mind a blank. I didn't want to think about what might happen today in the snow at Osmotherley. Yes, sometime between my arriving home early in the morning and getting up it had snowed – quite heavily too. There was a good three inches of white, coating the trees and garden. There was no sun but it looked a pleasant enough day.

By twelve o'clock I'd dug myself out of the drive and skidded and slithered up the bank out of the village onto the Thirsk–Northallerton road. The district council snow plough and gritting machines had been at work here and the road was clear into Northallerton. Kate Bishop was waiting for me and we made it spot on time, and conveniently found a parking spot just past the main gate.

We sat for a few minutes waiting for the professor to turn up. I put out my hand and covered Kate's.

"Let's put our heads into the church for a few minutes while we're waiting for Professor Stewart. Let's have a look at it in daylight."

We followed another set of footprints along the path between the gravestones, their outline blurred by the carpet of snow. Almost like making a prayer before embarking on something new, I thought as we entered the church. It looked much brighter than when lit by a few candles and light bulbs. We stood at the back holding hands, communicating with each other in another way – by finger pressure. The owner of the other footsteps in the snow was kneeling in a pew near the front. I looked a little more carefully. Surely I knew that back.

"Look," I whispered, "it's the professor."

We waited quietly, and after a few minutes he sat back on his seat, picked up his hat and gloves, and came down the aisle towards us.

"Hello, Tim. Hello, Kate."

"Professor, what are you doing?" I asked.

"I got here a couple of hours ago, Tim, and decided that I would get myself into mental trim for this exercise. So I've been doing a bit of what I asked you to do – meditation. Have you kept at it?"

"Yes, and with some startling results too."

"Oh?" He obviously hadn't expected to get anything out of it, so we'd had a bonus.

I explained in some detail how Kate had come with me each evening and what had happened on the Friday night.

Kate then went on and told him of our speculations during dinner at Bob's.

"Where is he?" He looked around.

"He's going to meet us at Osmotherley, as is Frank Cooper," I explained about Frank.

"Quite a band we're collecting together, aren't we?" He smiled. "A most unlikely band to be making history too, don't you think? Come on then, let's get on with it. Osmotherley first stop. We'll all go in my car, if you've no objections."

He didn't add "in case anything happened to me", but it hung on the air all the same.

Professor Stewart had never been to Mount Grace Priory. The entrance was just off the A19 to the right, about halfway between the junction of the Northallerton road with the A19 and the Tontine Inn. It just looked like a farm road leading away from the dual carriageway, near the bottom of the hill. The snow plough hadn't been up here, but a few tractors had and the snow had been packed in two basic wheel ruts which weren't difficult to drive in.

The best time to visit Mount Grace, I always think, is in the spring when the daffodils are out. The ruins against the backdrop of the woods look positively beautiful set in their carpet of green grass, decorated with splashes of yellow. But this Saturday was the fifth of December and today's carpet was a rich fluffy white one, which gave the ruins an air of ghostliness, their harsh outlines covered, and in some cases obliterated, by the snow.

Unlike the other mediaeval monastic orders in England, the Carthusians resembled hermits as much as they did monks. They lived in seclusion, not only from the world but also from each other. Most of the time the monk lived in isolation in his own cell to which his meals were brought, and inserted through a complicated little stone serving hatch to avoid contact. The major consequence of this philosophy of life was that the architecture of the priory was totally different from that of Fountains and Rievaulx. A communal dormitory was not needed, but an extensive cloister was necessary to fit in the individual cells with their little gardens.

We entered the priory through the gatehouse in the centre of the long range of buildings, forming the western side of the outer court. Today the custodian from the Department of the Environment had obviously decided that the chance of visitors was nil, which just goes to show how wrong one can be sometimes. There was, however, no problem about getting in and we walked almost on tiptoe across the outer court, leaving our trail in the virgin snow.

"Well, Jim," I asked the professor, "where do we do this experiment today? In the church ruins?"

"No, Tim. I think it would be best to do it in one of the cells. After all, that is where the real meditation was done. To go to the church was probably like having a day off and being let out into the world to meet other people. There probably wasn't much meditation done in there."

So we passed into the cloister, which had an odd irregular shape to it like a partly-folded quadrangle. The greater part of the enclosing wall still stood. Each cell stood in an angle of its garden adjoining the cloister wall. Some of them still stood almost complete, but others were shapeless mounds beneath the all-enveloping snow.

I indicated the cells. "Which one, Professor? Take your pick."

"I don't think it matters too much, Tim. I suggest you pick one which we can see into from out here, and we can keep away from you, but still keep an eye on you in case anything was to happen."

I could hear the sound of a car coming up the path from the main road. Its engine noise had separated from the general muffled, muted roar of traffic on the A19 dual carriageway.

"This could be Bob or Frank," I said. I had expected we would have lunch before coming here so I gave them both later times."

"Sorry to deprive you of your lunch, Tim, but part of a monk's training involved fasting.. You'll just have to pretend even harder that you are a monk. We'll have something to eat later," he promised.

It was Bob Atwell in his big wellington boots and leggings who ploughed through the snow to reach us.

"Right, are you ready, Tim?"

"Okay, Professor, here we go."

"Tim, be careful!" The last admonition came from Kate.

I scrambled over one of the low ruined walls into a cell space. I paused for a moment wondering whether I ought to stand in the cell space itself or in the garden area. Which space would the monk have used most? I came to the conclusion that it probably didn't matter, but from personal preference, if it had been me, I would have spent as much time as possible in the garden, so that is where I stood. I was standing in the garden of a cell which enabled me to stand looking to the east up the slopes of the wooded hillside. I took a deep breath to relax myself. Although it was a cold day I was well wrapped up and there was no wind, so I was warm enough. Facing east, as I was, I wasn't looking at my friends, so they couldn't distract me.

I started to concentrate, to put into effect what I'd been practising all week in Northallerton Church, and the practice paid off too, or maybe it was just the Mount Grace site. One moment I was looking out at the snow-covered hillside, the next that searing band of internal energy was taking me into myself again. I suddenly realised what I'd had in the pit of my stomach all week. It had been a gnawing sense of loss, but I hadn't been able to define it because I didn't know I had lost. Now, again, I realised what it was. It was this storehouse of knowledge to which I now had access. I was even able to identify now what this band of energy was, the source of the throbbing power that I'd felt on the previous occasions. It was unbelievably an internal communications system used for moving all this information around. I even found that I could control it. It was easy. I was over the threshold and with control came the power to filter it. I could eliminate the drumming and pulsating of the power and filter the information. I could call for large blocks or small blocks. The information was catalogued in a strange system, but as I became more expert with the manipulation I realised that the communications channel had literally thousands of channels for parallel processing of information. Then I felt a shock, a powerful signal from outside was trying to gain access. The sheer force of it almost took me back into the real world, but with an effort I hung on. It came again – a demand for access, a demand for information. Whatever, or whoever, was trying to gain access was also new at this control, but she was getting better – somehow I knew that it was a *she*. Softer and with more gentle accuracy, she tried to hook into my communications channel. Like the parallel highway of a powerful computer multiplexing vast amounts of data, this highway suddenly made a link up with my ordinary everyday world. My system realised that it was Kate who was trying to get in and gave her permission for access. It was a strange feeling allowing access to one's information to another person. For some reason my communications band did not extend outside myself and I could not transmit or receive these ethereal transmissions myself. I had to rely on Kate. I felt that I had the answers here to the questions we'd been asking ourselves, but there was so much and so little time to analyse it. Yes, Kate had asked the right question about teaching, and Bob had undoubtedly the answer. I needed some training to handle all this. My experience was insufficient: I couldn't control the flow. I panicked. I had all this but how could I use it. If I wasn't careful, it would be lost again. That made me panic worse. The external communications channel was suddenly stepping up its power-demanding attention, momentarily overriding my panic. It was putting out reassurance, but I wasn't able to complete the loop and I then lost control again. The drumming came back. I fought it hard for control. I steadied momentarily into the steady stream of pure energy I'd seen at Rievaulx. In a flash like lightning it leapt into the cosmos. The immensity of the universe suddenly lay before me. The planets and stars were but atoms in the interlacing whole. A whole without a beginning and without an end. For a fraction of an instant of human time I felt a glancing contact with another awareness. It would have been wrong to describe it as 'a being' in our terms. It wasn't a thing either. But before I could grasp out again, my waves of panic had grown again and were crashing in on me higher and higher. The throbbing grew and grew until in a deafening roar I lost contact again with that other me – the other me in the other two-thirds of my brain. Then a bleakness came over me, an overwhelming sense of loss. The hills were before my eyes again, the sky grey and threatening more snow. I was still on my feet – only just. I could feel myself swaying slightly, but I didn't care. I had lost... lost what? I couldn't remember. I wanted to cry, but that too seemed pointless. I'd forgotten what I was doing there surrounded by grey sandstone walls. An echo of that dark, other world, panic reached out to me and I toppled over, and for a time all my troubles left me. I blacked out completely.

*

The darkness about me, which I'd become aware of for some time, was slipping away. It was turning a grey colour and lightening further. I was very comfortable, lying on something soft and my head buried in something soft and warm. Funny, I hadn't realised that snow could be so comfortable. I remembered falling and thought I must be still lying in the snow. But it really was too warm for snow. They said that it was a comfortable way to die, lying in the snow. You just lost all feeling and gradually slipped away. But I wasn't slipping away. I was warm and comfortable but I could feel my hands and legs and toes against the sheets. Sheets! The greyness gave way to light but I still didn't open my eyes. If I was lying in the snow, the professor and Bob and Kate would reach me soon to pick me up. But I couldn't hear anything, just a soft indefinable murmur like the noise made by people working. I really was comfortable and didn't want to open my eyes to find out what was happening. I wanted to remain curled up in the warmth. Returning consciousness, however, began to overcome that and reluctantly I flicked one eye open and then the other, but I didn't move anything else. I was in a small room with a white ceiling and grey walls. I closed my eyes and opened them again. The room was still there and it had a window through which the sun was streaming. I identified the noise. It *was* the sound of people working. I was in hospital. The dawning awareness of that fact caused me to sit up in bed, or at least to try to. It was then that I realised that my head was bandaged. It was strange that I was in a room on my own and perhaps stranger that there was no one else in the room keeping an eye on me. I had obviously hurt myself when I had fallen but I would have thought that someone would have stayed with me – Kate, at least.

Suddenly there was some movement outside the door and it opened briskly and my hand was grasped. It wasn't Kate though, it was a nurse taking my pulse.

"Well, welcome back, Mr Drummond. How do you feel?"

I moved my head to look at the efficient nurse grasping my hand. I took in her light blue and white uniform before my head felt as though someone had dropped an anvil on it and I gasped out loud with the pain.

She reached out to hold my shoulders and encouraged me to hold my head still. I didn't need much encouragement to do that and gradually the anvil stopped ringing.

"Phew, sorry, Nurse."

She got hold of my hand again, smiling encouragingly. "It's Sister, actually. We might as well start as we mean to go on." The words were said brusquely and business-like but her smile belied her tone.

"I'll get the doctor," and before I could ask anything she'd gone.

It wasn't long before she returned with an elderly man a white coat.

"The doctor, I presume." I was very careful not to move my head.

"You presume right, young man. Doctor Barnes. You've had quite a nasty knock there."

"You can say that again," I agreed, moving my head ever so slowly and slightly to see if he had intentions of taking off the bandage. But he hadn't. He just pulled up a chair and sat down next to the bed. The sister stood deferentially behind him.

"How do you feel?"

"Apart from this hammer in here, not too bad."

He looked at me for a long time and eventually came to a decision with himself.

"Do you know what day it is?"

I looked at the window and the obvious morning sunshine. It looked as though I'd slept the night through for some reason. "Well. . . it could be Sunday," I suggested.

"It could be," he agreed, "but it isn't. You were admitted to this hospital on—"

"Saturday." I helped him out.

"Yes, quite correct," he agreed, "but that was Saturday, 5th of December. Today is Tuesday the 29th."

I was aghast. "You mean, I've lost nearly a month?" I suddenly had another thought. "It is *still* December, isn't it?" I asked a little weakly.

"Indeed it is. But yes," he answered my previous question, "you have lost a few weeks. I'm afraid you've been suffering from concussion. . ." he faltered, ". . .no, concussion is the wrong word. I'm afraid I don't know what it was exactly. You have nothing obviously wrong with your head apart from some cuts and bruises you got when you were thrown against a wall."

That explained the bandage.

"There's been something else." He viewed me. "We'll talk about that later though when Professor Stewart gets here."

"Where am I? Am I in Northallerton?"

"Oh, yes. We thought it best not to move you. You are in the Friarage Hospital."

"And is Professor Stewart here?"

"No, I'm afraid not, but I would think that by now he knows you are conscious again." He threw an interrogative glance across the room to the sister who responded with a nod.

"Yes, he'll be here for about eight o'clock this evening."

Have you—" I started to ask and she nodded again.

"Yes, Mr Drummond. Miss Bishop has also been informed." She glanced at her watch. "I would think that she'll be here any minute now."

For the next ten minutes the doctor continued to ask me questions about how I felt, while avoiding other questions from me.

The door opened and Kate flew in. She hadn't her usual poise and was somewhat flushed from hurrying. She stopped at the foot of the bed and our eyes joined hands. A look of relief passed across her face.

"It's all right, young lady. I'm pleased to say that Mr Drummond appears to respond quite normally. Now that he's come round, I would think that another week or two and he'll be out of here." He got up from the chair.

"Now, Miss Bishop, no more than twenty minutes this first time. I assume that you'll be coming back with Professor Stewart this evening."

"Yes, I will. Thank you very much, Doctor."

She waited until the door closed before she moved. By then she'd regained her composure.

I was still trying not to move my head as she took hold of my hands. For some minutes no conversation was possible. Eventually I took courage and asked, "Kate, what happened?" I was still staggered at losing four weeks of time.

"I don't know, Tim." She shook her head, her eyes troubled. "Honestly, I'd rather wait until Professor Stewart arrives."

"Is he coming from Sheffield?"

"Yes. He stayed for a week after it happened, but we had no means of knowing when you would come round. Or whether you would come round at all."

That first twenty minute visit fled by about ten times faster than the time was passing elsewhere, and she'd gone before I realised that I'd hardly had any hard information out of her. But I felt tired again and I began to slip away into sleep. I fought it at first, worried that I might not wake again, but gradually I gave up and I eventually dived into the pleasant waiting whirlpool of darkness.

The next thing I was aware of was a gentle pressure on my arm and a quite insistent voice, which dragged me up through the levels of unconsciousness until I opened my eyes to find the sister saying that it would soon be eight o'clock, and would I please have something to eat before my visitors arrived. It seemed to me that I was getting privileged treatment. Surely NHS patients didn't have dinner at this time of the evening?

By the time that Kate and the professor put in an appearance I had been spruced up and even propped up slightly in bed at the cost of a tremendous hammering from the blacksmith in my skull.

The professor came in full of concern and his handshake was longer than the usual hello.

"You were right, Kate, he *is* himself," he said finally.

"Did you think I wouldn't be?"

"Let's face it, you haven't been for the last few weeks," he answered.

"Please, please." I made a weak attempt to hold up my hands. "Tell me what happened."

"Can't you remember?"

""No, Jim, I can't. I do remember walking into the monk's cell and I looked up the hillside, but then it went dark except. . ." I remembered a strange feeling.

"Yes," prompted the professor.

". . .except that I do remember falling, and cracking my head."

"Some fall. You don't realise—"

"Professor!" Kate stopped him. "It would be better if we started at the beginning."

"Yes, of course, my dear. You tell him." A look passed between them across the bed.

"As you've said, Tim, you went into the cell at Mount Grace and stood with your back to us. We just watched you for a few minutes and then the professor suggested that it might be some help if I could communicate with you. So I very quietly - which was easy because of the snow - joined you in the little garden. I walked around in front of you and stopped." Kate wasn't looking at me now she was staring out of the window. In reality she wasn't even doing that: she was reliving those minutes up at Mount Grace.

". . .I faced you and closed my eyes. Tim, it was much easier than in Northallerton Church. How it happens I have no idea, but I could 'feel' your thoughts and I called to be let in. It must be distance-related though, because I could feel you shrink away. I tried a few more times and then it happened - I merged into your mind, Tim. You let me in, but you didn't come into mine. Can you honestly not remember?"

I held on tightly to her hands as I desperately tried to remember. No, I couldn't. There was the faintest of echoes struck, but nothing positive.

"No, Kate," I whispered. "Go on."

But Kate was overcome with the memory and the professor took over to let her recover.

"Kate was able to tap into your storehouse of knowledge, Tim. She described later to us how you had a voyage of discovery through all this information. Much more, much more than you could possibly have learned in your lifetime. You raced through it at a vast speed, not holding any of it long enough to study, but Kate was so bewildered by it that she's had great difficulty keeping up with you."

"Yes, Tim, you were like an excited little boy let loose among a huge number of new toys. You didn't know what to do with them all.

Suddenly it all became too much for you and you panicked. You fought to control it, almost recovered control, and then something happened. I had a glimpse of some vast incomprehensible power, but just a glimpse because you suddenly closed me out. It was more like throwing me out and away from you." Tears had appeared in Kate's eyes. "I came to in normal surroundings to see you flying back through the air to crash your head against the wall."

"You mean, I *didn't* fall?"

"You certainly didn't," broke in the professor.

"This whole business probably took about twenty minutes or so, during which time your friend, Frank Cooper, arrived and we quietly introduced ourselves. Suddenly you catapulted backwards away from Kate as though you'd been hit hard. You crashed violently into the wall – hence the bandage," he nodded to my head. "But you can't remember? Not even now we've told you?" He had a faintly hopeful look.

"No, Jim, I can't."

Conversation stopped while an auxiliary nurse brought in a tray of tea, but there was nothing wrong with my mind now, it raced along. I let her leave the room and close the door.

"But if Kate can remember what happens and can go with me on these trips into my subconscious, surely we can make progress. Each time we can get more information. Eventually we both may be able to use the same facilities together, instead of separately as they are at the moment.

"Steady on, Tim, you've only just recovered from the last one, you aren't ready for another go yet." Kate was concerned, but the professor was trying not to show that I'd just made his day.

"We thought you mightn't want to risk it again, Tim."

"But Professor, that's what we agreed to do, isn't it?"

"Yes, but your head—"

"Well, okay, it hurts a bit now, but it'll get better, won't it?"

"It should have been better two weeks ago, Tim," said the professor dryly. "But I must admit something strange has kept you unconscious for a long time. Something inexplicable by ordinary medicine. Fair enough you did have a crack on the head, but it wasn't as bad as all that."

"Never mind that, Professor, we obviously have to make another trial. Where is it to be next time?"

"Look, Tim, you should recover from—"

"Professor, I won't believe you if you say you haven't thought about the next step. Come on, what is it?"

He continued to protest concern, but you could tell that he was ready to continue with his plans as soon as possible, and after a little more formal persuasion he proposed the next course of action.

"After we'd brought you in to hospital here I had quite a long chat with your friend, Frank, and we discussed what Kate told us. It is obvious that we have to have a look at some of this store of information you have. So far we have come up with no theory as to why or how you have so much stored knowledge. Frank described what happened at Housesteads again and he pointed out that that was a much older site and you had a specific experienced. You went back physically or mentally in time and became a Roman soldier."

"You are suggesting reincarnation, Professor?"

"No, I'm not, Tim, though it might account for that level of knowledge. Let us try to keep an open mind for now until we have some more to work on."

"Frank also pointed out that you remembered what had happened, Tim," Kate emphasised the point. She desperately wanted me to remember – perhaps even more than I did myself.

"Yes, I'd forgotten that, Kate – Frank did emphasise that, didn't he? That could tie up with selecting and exploring one piece or area of knowledge that might aid remembrance."

"Come to the point, Professor, please." My head was aching again and I was having some difficulty in following him.

"Right, I will. When we get you out of here, our next test site should be a prehistoric site and we'll try to get you to stop and pick out knowledge related to that site or at least that point in time."

"Have you thought how you'll exercise this control?" I asked, pointing out that as I couldn't relate my day-to-day mind to my sub-mind, I was highly unlikely to be able to control the information I looked at.

"Using Kate," was his simple reply. It fitted together quite neatly.

"And where is this to take place, and when?"

"The *when* depends on you, Tim. You have to recover properly first before we dare try again. The *where*..." He hesitated and put his hand into his inside pocket.

"I didn't want it to be a popular site like Stonehenge. I'm sure it might be a very potent location, but it has a lot of tourists which might disturb it. In any case, it would be better to have a place near here somewhere."

"Is there anywhere?" I asked.

Oh, yes, indeed. I've had a good look through all the books during the last few weeks. Here. . ." He handed me a photograph. It was an aerial photograph.

"Can you see those three circles?"

The photograph was a typical patchwork of fields with a farmhouse. In the centre of the picture, Clearly visible, was a circle taking up well over half of the field. Higher up the picture in another field, two fields away, was another circle, but I couldn't see the third and I said so.

"See that wood." He pointed at the trees in the bottom of the photograph. "It's there."

I looked very carefully and could see the circle in the trees.

"Those three circles are in a dead straight line north-west to south-east. Each one is about eight hundred feet in diameter with entrances north-west and south-east, and they are about half a mile apart. Each has a massive bank, originally about ten feet high, with a ditch inside and outside it, about sixty-five feet wide and about ten feet deep. The outer ditches, as you can see from that photograph, have been filled up by ploughing."

"How old are they?" I asked.

"Well, the books I've read put them about 1700 to 1400 BC."

"So, about three and half thousand years."

"Yes, Tim, but first of all you have to get better."

"Yes, Kate, but that won't take long and this gives me something to get better for. Whereabouts is it, Professor?" He took the photograph from my hand.

"It's not far away, Tim. It's about five miles north of Ripon. They are called The Thornborough Circles."

Chapter Eleven

The Thornborough Circles

It was, however, some time before I was allowed out of hospital. As the old year died and we slipped into the new one, slowly, very slowly, the pain in my head eased until I could move it with only the slightest of pain. I found out why I was in a private room. Professor Stewart had alerted his contacts in governmental circles to what we were doing and I had fallen under the protective mantle of the British Government. Hence the private room. We weren't being interfered with in any way, but a cabinet minister had the remit to keep himself informed of our activities. These activities were restricted for somewhat longer than I had anticipated, by the insistence of the hospital authorities in trying to find out what the problem with my head really was. I suffered an almost continuous series of tests.

I wasn't the only one champing at the bit, of course. The professor did his best not to show his impatience, but it showed all the same. When he came to visit me, his restless prowling around the room and continuous fiddling with pencils and pens gave the game away.

Finally, however, the day came when the doctors gave up and pronounced me fit again. It was the last Sunday in January before Kate came to collect me from the hospital and I began to take up my life again. I felt a bit cheated that I'd missed Christmas, but then I'd missed most of the snow too, and on the day I came out it was almost spring-like, and as if to prove it the days were beginning to lengthen.

I had another week off work, but took up the reins again after the first week in February. I had a lot of sympathy and questions asked in the first few days back at work. A lot of people were answered in a vague unsatisfactory way as to what had been the matter with me. After a few days people got used to me being around again and though not satisfied they stopped asking the questions. Bob Atwell was my mainstay in this period. Without appearing to at all, he managed to lead lunchtime conversations into other channels. He playfully pushed and prodded people into other conversations and arguments. Sometimes it was impossible to tell if Bob was being completely serious about the subject under discussion for he often became quite vehement about things. Regularly he stirred people into serious arguments and then suddenly backed off with a sudden disarming grin.

By mid-February my first week at work had had no adverse impact or effects on my head, so I declared myself ready to proceed to the Thornborough experiment.

It was to be a similar party to that which went to Mount Grace. Frank Cooper was coming down from Newcastle and was going to pick up Bob Atwell en route. We were going to meet at the circles. Professor Stewart was also coming up from Sheffield. As the afternoons were lengthening a little we decided to meet at two o'clock near the middle circle. We had all acquired a copy of the ordinance survey map No. 91 for the Ripon area, so we were all convinced that despite never having been there before, we would all find them easily enough.

Kate called for me just after one o'clock and we drove towards Thirsk and crossed the River Swale at Skipton, hitting the A1 the other side of Ainderby Quernhow. I'd never been on this road before and was surprised to find that it crossed the A1 by passing under it. After a few miles we found the road sign for Thornborough and turned into the narrow village road. A sharp dog-leg turn past the telephone box brought us into the tiny village of stone and cobble cottages. Following the road out of the village, according to my map, would bring us to the centre circle. All the way from the A1 the land was typical Vale of York – flat with lots of cultivated fields, and to the west the land began to rise towards Masham.

The road had a small hedge on each side, making it easy to see from the car. Soon we came to a field entrance about where I judged we should find the circles. Kate pulled in to the side and we got out. As yet no one else had arrived, and as we walked to the gap in the hedge only the birds disturbed the stillness. I stood in the gate and looked to the north-west. We were spot on. The great central circle could be clearly picked out, its earthworks covered in grass, rising above the level of the field in a series of irregular mounds of varying heights, some as high as ten feet. Behind it I could see the farmhouse and behind that the wood which concealed another circle. The aerial photograph which the professor had shown me was clearly recognisable here on the ground. It was of course much more difficult to see the whole pattern. I crossed the road and looked over the hedge to see if I could see the third circle, but it was obscured by the rise and fall of the land. I went back and leaned on the car again, close to Kate. For a time we said nothing. We felt almost like intruders on this silent landscape. For thousands of years these circles had been here. That of itself was quite an incredible thought.

"What are circles for, Tim?" Kate was the first to throw a pebble into the sea of silence.

"I don't know, Kate. No one really knows what they were for."

"But surely someone must know. The countryside is littered with them, isn't it?"

"It is, yes, but I think that though people have written a lot about them and done much theorising about them, their true purpose remains lost in the mists of time."

A car engine could be heard approaching and a minute or two later we were joined at the gate by Professor Stewart.

"So it's here." He nodded towards the mound.

"Yes, Professor, I was just asking Tim what all these circles were about."

"And no doubt he's told you we don't know."

"Well, he has," she nodded, "but I still can't believe that with all our modern techniques we can't find out what they were about."

"Yes, it is rather tantalising, isn't it?" Professor Stewart wasn't restless today. He was back at work again and could afford to savour the experience. He leaned on the car too while we awaited the arrival of Bob and Frank.

"In the past few years there have been a lot of people doing a lot of work on circles. They've measured them, theorised about their geometry, related them to astronomy and so on, but they're no nearer knowing what they were for."

"Do we know how old they are?"

"Well, we do have an idea from carbon dating."

"Oh! I've heard of that, but I haven't a clue what it means. Do you know, Tim?"

"I do, yes. It's a form of dating done using a radioactive isotope of carbon. It's called carbon-14 and this material is derived when nitrogen atoms in the air are struck by cosmic rays. When carbon combines with oxygen to form carbon dioxide, some of the carbon atoms are those of carbon-14. Now, plants and trees absorb carbon dioxide, and men and animals too, when they eat plants. When they die, they don't absorb any more, so if we measure the amount of carbon-14 still present in bones and fibres taken from sites like this one we can get a measure of its age."

"That sounds very complicated to me," said Kate. "How did you know that?"

"We deal with radioactive materials at work, actually. We use them in some instruments."

"But I believe there is some problem with carbon dating, isn't there?" asked Professor Stewart.

"I don't know, Professor. I don't honestly know much about it."

"Neither do I really," he admitted, "but I've been reading up a bit about it in view of our experiments."

"So what's the problem with it?" asked Kate.

"I understand that recent research has shown that carbon-14 years become increasingly younger than true calendar years. That means that for something dated in the fourth millennium BC, the true date of the sample could be seven hundred years older than its carbon-14 date."

"What does that mean, Professor? What effect does it have on circles?"

"Well, Kate, it would mean that some of them, like Stonehenge, were constructed several centuries before the Mycenaean civilisation from whose architectural experience the builders had been thought to have drawn."

"That's the first time I've heard that, Professor. Does that have an impact on what we are going to do?"

The professor shrugged his shoulders. "If it's true, it could have, but since we don't know very well what we're looking for we can't say what effect it's going to have."

He turned from the car to watch another approaching car, which turned out to be Frank and Bob.

"Come on then, let's get moving."

We walked up the field side towards where the circle intersected it, thus avoiding walking over the ploughed field to one of the entrances to the circle. There were two entrances to it, one at each side in a line with the other two circles. We climbed the mound and found ourselves looking across the wide interior of the circle. It was surprisingly large, about eight hundred feet across with the mound complete all the way round, but of varying heights. The area in the centre had been ploughed, but the outer mound was covered with grass and gorse bushes.

"Right, now this is the plan today." The professor took charge and we all gathered round to listen.

"We know that under certain circumstances Tim can gain access to immense stores of knowledge, but he cannot consciously remember them later. Coincidentally, Kate here is able somehow to attune herself mentally with Tim and follow his thought processes, and she is able to remember what happened afterwards. So the idea is that Tim, under prodding from Kate, will go back to the period in time when these circles were built and she will, we hope, relay any information that Tim has stored about this period. Let's not make it any more complicated than that for the moment. Are you ready, Tim?"

"Yes, Jim."

Everyone was ignoring the possible consequences, everyone that is except Kate. She along with the others remembered the violent conclusion to our last experiment. She held my arm.

"Tim, you don't have to go into this thing, you know. If you want to, we can all just go home."

"No, Kate." I took her hand off my arm and pushed her away. "It's too late to back out now. Let's get on." We left the mound and picked our way across the central area to the exact middle of the circle.

I had not entirely wasted my time in the hospital. It had been an ideal place to practise meditation. In fact several times I'd been so successful that the sister had thought that I'd had a relapse.

I faced Kate, about three feet separating us, and held her eyes with mine for a few seconds before I closed mine. Together this time we concentrated. Incredibly, it was easy, much easier than at Mount Grace. The professor had certainly got it right about these ancient religious sites being powerful focusing points.

I had immediate control of the communications channel and almost immediately I sensed, rather than felt, Kate's signal. She too had better control this time. She was able to gauge it much better and when she asked for access it wasn't like the shock I'd received previously. I almost automatically allowed her to communicate.

At first I experimented myself. Yes, I could still retain control of the normal part of my everyday brain. To prove it I opened my eyes and looked straight into Kate's face three feet away. She smiled and nodded. She of course knew what I was doing. I closed them again and didn't actually need Kate to tell me that I was looking for information relating to a period around fourteen to seventeen hundred years BC. I began to search, dipping into large blocks of information – some of it vague, some of it specific. Back through the centuries into the dark ages, but knowledge was still there. In some generations, the knowledge was scant and superficial. It came and went in waves. It had a vast amount of detail about the British Roman period. For a few seconds or so it seemed to me, I sifted some of the memories in this period and, sure enough, there it was. I was a British Roman citizen. I remembered one of my postings, from my base in the city Eboracum, was to Housesteads on the wall built by the Emperor Hadrian. Yes, I could remember going to the Mithraic Temple near the fort. I didn't really believe in Mithras of course, but it was politic to go to the temple from time to time. There was law, there was peace, there was order, food, warmth, culture and learning. The population was free from barbarism. In fact from my brief glimpses on the way back, Britain was a good place to live in then – better than at many periods during the ensuing centuries.

Kate was getting a little impatient. Seventeen hundred years BC, she reminded me. So back I went further in time. Information still abounded. It was just as easy to get at, but it was now stored in a different way. I was in a different part of the brain. Here it was very dense with memory cells. Access was restricted to a sort of bulk storage method. One could almost equate it to disc storage on a computer. To look at it, it had to be brought forward a level where it could be split up and assimilated. It wasn't a problem handling it though, the delay was negligible, but there were generations of information in each package. Glimpses of wars and invasions and strange tribes. Throughout all of this strange journey back through time there was always the thread of location. Most of the time I was in the north of the land we now call England. Occasionally journeys were made elsewhere, but usually I was somewhere in the north.

Suddenly I had a glimpse of a familiar-looking landscape. I felt Kate surge too. Yes, I was in the area of Thornborough and I was about two thousand five hundred years BC. I filtered the package more carefully and brought it into a higher level of my brain.

"What is it?" whispered Kate, except she didn't really whisper it. For the first time she'd imposed direct conversation into my conscious mind because she was so excited at what I was seeing.

Gone was the familiar structure of the fields, but I was standing in an area which had been completely cleared of trees. It was an oblong area, perhaps two miles long by half a mile wide. Outside that the forest seemed to be unbroken. In front of me was one of the circles, but its walls were high, about fifteen feet, and it had a wide ditch around it filled with water. A broad space about forty feet wide separated the walls from the ditch. The wall was coated with a blazing white colour. A flat smooth road went into the circle. In fact, it went out of the other side too. I turned and looked to the north-west and sure enough the road came from another circle in a dead straight line. I had no doubt that if I walked around the other side of the circle it would carry on in a straight line to the third circle. The road was very smooth – in fact, it looked like a form of concrete. It was in sharp contrast to the earthworks around the circle.

I searched my memory to find a record of a time when I'd been inside the circle. But at first I didn't find it. The place was obviously a sacred structure. In each of the circles there was a stone structure... or was it stone? My old memory hadn't a name for it. Over the years I joined in the ceremonies at the circle. They were always held at night, but the whole place was always bathed in light, not from the flickering torches which lit our homes, but from the four great pillars standing around the building. The light was as strong as daylight. Whenever dusk approached, the white light illuminated this forest clearing. It had happened for years as long as anyone could remember. No one lit them: they just happened. But our priests said that they were built by the strange gods centuries and centuries before. In puzzlement I tried to go further back, but the effort was becoming greater. There was information there, even more densely packed. To sort that out would need a much greater effort. So instead I came forward a little and came across a memory.

I was in a vast tunnel lined with lights. The lights were similar to those which illuminated the outside. Yes, I realised that I was inside the road. It ran for the two miles between the outer circles. There were no people around though. It was frighteningly quiet except for a hum. I didn't know where that came from, but I was determined to see where these gods lived. I found a stairway, but this was made out of something thin and strange. Nothing at all like our stone steps. I ventured down them and came onto a sort of balcony overlooking a huge altar – well, that's what I took it to be at first. I leaned forward to look across, and my head crashed into an invisible material. I looked more carefully I could see it if I looked carefully, but more importantly *I could see through it*. I could see the great round altar with strange structures around it and all sorts of coloured lights.

But now I was so tired that the effort to sort these memories was tremendous. Kate was calling to me to come back. There was a hum now from my communications channel similar to that first time. It was becoming stressed, and so as a last effort I transferred this last memory, this last block of information, not back into its file but up through the neuronal structure to the everyday section of the brain. I had to take something back with me into my world. If I could succeed, I would at least have some conscious idea of what was inside the cortex.

I felt cold as I opened my eyes. I had been well wrapped up when we came out this afternoon, but I was nearly numb with cold. I looked at Kate and as I did so her eyes flicked open and we fell into each other's arms, our teeth chattering. Both of us were trembling furiously.

There was a shout and Frank came running.

"Are you okay, Tim?" he shouted.

I nodded between my shivers.

We both turned to Kate. "And you, Kate?"

"Yes, I think so, but I'm absolutely frozen. What time is it, Frank?" She looked around. "Where are the others?"

Frank looked a little guilty. "It's five o'clock, actually, and we've been taking turns to stand guard over you both. Here come the others now. They've been sitting in the car. It's been so cold. Come on, let's get you across to the cars."

We met the professor and Bob Atwell halfway across the field.

"Are you both okay?" It was nice that he asked after us before he asked if we'd learnt anything. He even suggested that we got back to my cottage before we discussed anything. So it was an hour later when we'd all thawed out in my centrally heated cottage, with some drink to fortify us, before we got down to the post-mortem.

The professor, as usual, acted as chairman, posing the questions, sorting the information, probing and suggesting.

"Kate, I think that you should start this one off. I gather from your few comments that you have been successful in staying with Tim through this trial."

Kate nodded and smiled at me. "Yes, Professor, I was successful in communicating fully with Tim. Unfortunately, so far it is all communication on my part. Tim, although allowing it to happen, does not try to communicate with me." She looked at me a little sadly.

"Just before Kate starts, do you think I could ask Tim a question?" Bob Atwell was being very formal tonight.

The professor nodded. "If it's relevant, yes."

"Oh, certainly it is relevant, Professor." He turned to me as he tried to push his fingers into his waistcoat pockets again. Unfortunately he wasn't wearing a waistcoat, but he never noticed.

"Can you remember anything of what happened in the circle this afternoon, Tim?"

I'd realised for some time – in fact, since my teeth had stopped chattering – that the infuriating grey black wall had slammed down again.

"No, Bob, I can't remember a single thing."

"So, Kate, it all depends on you. What happened?"

Kate took a deep breath and started. "You have to realise that what I'm going to say might sound like a fairy story to you, but I assure you that it was taken from Tim's mind. It may be incomplete, because I didn't understand what was going on some of the time, but I'll do my best." And she did just that. She held us all spellbound for an hour and a half. No one spoke, we hardly breathed. We all followed my and Kate's journey into my brain with avid concentration, but still I couldn't remember anything of it. That is until she started talking about the tunnel under the circles and the description of the stairs and balcony and the room with the circular altar with the flashing lights.

I was aware of a dim recollection, bells were ringing louder and louder. From the fringes of my conscious memory I could see pictures flitting around in the greyness. Kate finished talking,

". . .and I'm sorry that I can't be clearer than that, but it seemed to me to be some sort of high technology."

"It was a nuclear pile cap."

The memory had rocketed forward into my present. I spoke the words and put my hands to my face. I couldn't believe it myself. Everyone in the room looked at me in absolute amazement.

It was Frank who recovered first.

"You have remembered then, Tim?"

I cast around in my mind for something of the other things that Kate had been talking about. I shook my head. "Yes and no, Frank. I can remember very clearly that image of the pile cap, but nothing else."

"How did you know it was a pile cap, Tim?" Professor Stewart brought us all back to order with his soft highland voice.

"It was a pile cap, I'm sure. You see, I worked on the commissioning of Wylfa Nuclear Power Station in Anglesey, and was involved in the initial designs for the computer control of the Hartlepool AGR Station."

"A nuclear power station beneath the Thornborough Circles." Bob was shaking his head. It wasn't often that Bob was lost for words, but at this instant he was. Frank however wasn't. He too had worked on nuclear stations.

"What kind of station was it, Tim? Have you any idea?" That was an interesting question. I appraised the memory and didn't quite believe the information I was producing. I shook my head in disbelief. Frank thought I was shaking it in the negative.

"That's a pity, it might have—"

"No, I didn't mean that, Frank. You are not going to believe this." I looked from one to the other.

The professor sat calmly well back in his armchair, his hands for once still. After all, he was getting some real hard, positive results for the first time. Bob Atwell, red-faced and sweating slightly now, mopped his brow nervously with a bundled handkerchief. Frank Cooper sat forward on the edge of his seat, every bit the professional systems analyst, drawing out every last known detail from the situation just as he would if he was preparing a flow diagram for one of his computer systems. Kate was the only one who I was sure would believe me with no reservations whatsoever – after all, she had been closer to me almost than I had been with myself.

"I think it was a fusion reactor." That really did shake Frank's cool and Bob mopped his brow faster.

"I don't understand, Tim. What does that mean?" It was Frank who explained to Kate.

"All the nuclear power stations in operation today, whatever method they use, are fission reactors. That means that they use a fissionable material like uranium-235, which decays if its nucleus is struck by a neutron. This nucleus vibrates, splits into two and ejects two or three neutrons at a high speed. If these neutrons are in a mass of uranium-235, they in turn will strike other nuclei and a chain reaction will commence with a tremendous release of energy. The unregulated chain reaction is called an atom bomb. A regulated one is a nuclear reactor. Another material used is plutonium-239. This is used in the type of developed experimental station which we are trying to build now. But Tim has suggested it was a fusion reactor. A fusion reactor does not yet exist and is unlikely to until well into the twenty-first century."

"But why?"

"Just hang on, Kate." Bob Atwell held his hand up. "Frank is going to tell us. You managed fission very well, Frank, see if you can keep fusion simple too,"

Frank allowed himself a tiny smile at the thought of fusion being simple.

"In a fusion reactor we are concerned with the fusion of the nuclei of the lightest element, hydrogen, into those of heavier elements. There are various reactions possible, but one of them uses deuterium, which is an isotope of hydrogen containing a proton and a neutron. If the nuclei of deuterium atoms are bombarded with the nuclei of other deuterium atoms, the deuterium nucleus may fuse with the proton from the other deuterium nucleus producing a nucleus of two protons and one neutron, i.e. the element helium. The spare neutron moves away at high speed with the conversion of the difference in mass into a vast amount of energy. An example of this uncontrolled reaction is the hydrogen bomb. Unfortunately, as yet, no one has come up with a controlled reaction."

"But why?"

"Because, my dear Kate, the temperature needed to create the conditions for this reaction is anything between about fifty million to three hundred million degrees centigrade."

"But, Tim, that's a colossal temperature."

I nodded in agreement.

"Yes, we think it might be found in the stars. We know it's created in an hydrogen bomb by exploding an atom bomb inside it."

Kate was now out of her depth and the professor getting that way. He made a valiant effort to recover.

"So what is the incentive to build fusion reactors?"

"The sea." Bob Atwell snapped out the two words, and Frank nodded in confirmation. "Yes, the sea. You see, Professor, deuterium can be obtained in virtually unlimited quantities from sea water, so we would have plenty of fuel available."

Frank sat back and pointed his index finger at me. "How or why did you think it was a fusion reactor, Tim?"

"It's a difficult question to answer, Frank, but there was a mimic diagram on the console in that balcony. It showed the process in some detail and it had what looked like a vast toroidal field coil surrounding the reactor."

"You mean, they had evolved a magnet powerful enough to isolate the hot plasma reaction away from the reactor walls?" Bob was overawed at the implied achievement. Even our modern technology had yet to achieve that prodigious feat.

The professor ventured a conclusion. "Do you mean, Tim, that these people, of a time approximately two thousand five hundred BC, could build something we can't do today?"

"No, I don't think that is my conclusion, Professor." I'd had a few minutes while Frank had been speaking to come up with a snap theory.

"I don't think that the people I am. . ." - I stopped a moment confused - "I mean, the people I *was*. . . had that capability. I think it was technology left over from an earlier people. A lost race - perhaps a race of gods."

Chapter Twelve
The Gods

"Yes. . . it's possible," nodded Bob Atwell in that sudden confident and surprising way he had.
"I've read various theories that there has been a technological race before this one."
"Can you remember anything you've read about it, Bob?"
"If I think about it for a minute or two I should be able to," confirmed Bob. "It's one of those things that has intrigued me for a long time, and as a result I've picked up and read odd articles from time to time that other so-called logical people might have not bothered with as being impossible."

He looked at the ceiling for a minute or two, while we waited, giving him time to think. He had an embarrassed grin on his face, almost as though he was going to tell us something we wouldn't believe.

"Look. . . just let's set the scene," he emphasised the point by holding his hands wide apart.

"For several hundred years now the conventional historians have been asserting that modern man is the result of an evolutionary process which began millions of years ago. They stick to those theories despite the fact that they cannot draw the veil of history back from much further than six thousand years. They could have fallen into the trap that many experts fall into—"

"If it isn't within their common experience or knowledge, it is impossible." Frank explained the trap in a single sentence.

Bob nodded. "That's it, Frank. Many eminent scientists have said that something is impossible only to be proven wrong in a very short space of time. My philosophy is that nothing is impossible. If you think it's impossible, then it only requires the application of time, money and effort and it will become possible. If someone somewhere wants something hard enough, it can be made to happen. But I'm getting away from my point." Bob always had a tendency to explain, at length, side issues, but they were usually interesting in themselves.

"What if modern man isn't the result of an evolution, but something else?"

"For example, this thing I've got about the brain only using one third of its capacity and the consequent question: what is or was the rest of it for?"

"Yes, exactly, Tim. But don't side-track me again." He paused for a breath.

"Over the years there has been information gathered at various historical and archaeological sites that have been totally unexplained by the conventional historian. For example, as long ago as the 1850s a metallic vase was dynamited out of solid rock in Massachusetts. The body resembled zinc material and it had very delicate inlaid silver work carved into it. Where did it come from? As far as the archaeologists were able to estimate, the rock from which it was taken was several million years old.

Bob was a surprising person. For a mechanical engineer he knew the strangest things. He had a sort of vacuum cleaner capacity for sucking in all sorts of miscellaneous fragments, mostly useless pieces of information. He continued disgorging some of them.

"In the 1880s a small metal cube was discovered in a coal seam in Austria. The edges of the cube were exactly straight and sharp. Four of the sides were flat and the other two opposite each other were convex. A deep groove was cut all the way around the cube. There was little doubt that it was machine-made and part of a larger mechanism. How did it get into the coal seam?"

Bob was warming to the subject now and he dredged up another example.

"There was a find by some divers working off a Greek island on the remains of a ship dated between eighty and fifty BC. Among the find was a lump of corroded bronze and wood. It was found in about 1900, I think, but it wasn't until the 1950s that it was discovered what it was. It was a very intricate miniature planetarium that calculated the rising and setting times of the moon and planets with a remarkable · accuracy.

"You know, there are lots and lots of these examples. Oh. . ." – Professor Stewart had been about to interrupt him, but Bob held his finger up – "...this one is perhaps nearer to what Tim has been talking about.. There was an archaeologist in Baghdad just before the Second World War, and he was rummaging in the basement of a museum when he came across some two-thousand-year-old clay pots from an excavation. On examination, each one was six inches high and enclosed a cylinder of copper. There were also iron rods suspended in the centre of the copper cylinders, which had been corroded away. They were, in fact, electric cells. Electroplated objects have been found in Babylonian ruins dating back to two thousand years BC, and also in Egyptian ruins. It undeniably all points to an earlier technological age."

"But what happened to it?" I'm sure it was the question rising to everyone's lips, but Kate asked it first.

"Do you have a theory, Bob?"

"There are of course all sorts of theories, though some of them are not really tenable; but you might be interested in one or two of them." He paused, almost embarrassed at holding the floor for so long.

"I think that to have wiped it out so completely there must have been some sort of natural catastrophe. It could have been a war, a nuclear war, but you would expect to find some signs of that, and there aren't any. So you come back to a natural catastrophe, and there *is* a record of such a worldwide catastrophe. It crops up in many legends in many parts of the world—"

"Noah's flood."

"Yes, Professor, the flood. It is believed that the flood is an historical fact."

"But, Bob, if there was a technological society at that point in time, it could have survived – it should have had the knowledge."

"No, not necessarily, Frank." Bob's hands sought his non-existent waistcoat pockets again.

"In theory yes, but a technological society is dependent on a large population for its maintenance and specialisation. Knowledge and detail are spread through many people. The legends associated with the flood tell us that very few people survived. It in unlikely that those few people would be able to support the technology, and so it gradually but surely died out. Instead of being centres of technology these places became centres of worship, because things happened there that they didn't understand, so they worshipped them and ascribed their activities to the gods."

"You mean, these ceremonies that I've described Tim taking part in were in fact worshipping a fusion reactor?" There was near incredulity in Kate's voice.

"It's only my theory," admitted Bob, "but it fits. Look, it's fantastic that you can sit inside Tim's mind and watch him slide back through thousands of years. You expect us to believe that it actually happens, don't you?" He asked Kate the question directly.

"But it does happen, Bob, it *does*."

"Okay, I believe you, but *you* have to keep an open mind too."

Before they got too seriously entangled Professor Stewart diplomatically intervened.

"I think I can accept what Bob is postulating. Tim, when you went into this reactor building, Kate said that there was no one around."

I nodded, looking to Kate for confirmation.

"Yes." She too nodded. "There was only the hum, but no people."

"Presumably the hum of the electrical generators," said Frank.

"From what I can remember of the reactor floor control room, it looked to be a fully automatic plant," I added to the building pile of evidence.

"It would have to be fully automatic for a fusion reactor, Tim, wouldn't it? You wouldn't be able to rely on any manual intervention in a process like that."

"True, Frank. Just think of the safety systems we put in a modern chemical plant and the triplicated voting systems in modern nuclear power stations. To run a fusion process must involve a tremendous safety problem."

There was quiet in the room for some minutes as we all envisaged a pre-history technological civilisation more advanced than our own that had been virtually wiped out by a natural catastrophe which left only a few survivors, survivors who weren't able to operate the technology but only to use it. Use it perhaps for hundreds of years, but gradually it wore out and stopped operating, and civilisation was set back thousands of years, slipping back slowly into the darkness and having to evolve from nothing again.

Kate was first to break into our thoughts. "If we were to dig under the Thornborough Circles would we find this technology now?"

"I'd wondered that too," nodded the professor. Frank Cooper also had thought about it for he had an answer. Where Bob Atwell knew a lot about lots of strange things, Frank Cooper always went into his work in great detail, and as he'd worked on nuclear power it was one of his great interests.

"No, I don't think we'd find anything."

"Nothing, Frank?"

"No, Professor, I'm afraid not. The biggest difficulty in operating a fusion reactor is to hold the plasma from contact with any material thing, because of its temperature. I've thought about what Tim described as the control room, and I think that it may well have operated totally automatically for hundreds of years, supplying power to illuminate that clearing and do many other innumerable things. In fact, as there are three circles at Thornborough, it is likely that there were three reactors, all connected by an underground tunnel. No matter how many safety systems there were protecting the reactors, without regular maintenance eventually something would go wrong. With no technologists to maintain them, one by one they would shut down automatically, depending on the type of fault. But with three reactors the odds must be pretty good that one of the toroidal magnetic systems would fail eventually and—"

"You'd get a colossal melt-down, wouldn't you?"

"Yes, Bob, something like that. A plasma at such a fantastic temperature suddenly released would cause the total destruction by heat of the power station, and that would easily encompass the other reactors whether they were working or not. It would fuse the whole of the ground in that area into a solid piece of rock."

"But the radioactivity?" questioned Bob. "Surely present-day reactors take thousands of years to lose their radioactivity. In that case we should have been able to detect it even now."

"Yes, that would have been true, Bob, if it had been like ours, a fission reactor, but the level of radioactivity from a fusion reactor would be negligible."

"Very neat, Frank, very neat," nodded Professor Stewart. "You've accounted for the disappearance of everything except a few mounds still standing around the circles, and, depending how deep the reactors were, it is feasible that that would happen. But you're wrong, you know, when you say that nothing would remain underground of this complex that Tim and Kate have described."

We all looked at him in some surprise.

"I haven't told anyone about this until now, but, as is my habit, I've been reading everything I could find about the Thornborough Circles in the last few weeks while we've been waiting for Tim's recovery. If you remember, I showed Tim a picture of the Thornborough Circles when he was in hospital – this one." He showed it to us again. "But under certain conditions of crop on the land you can quite clearly see a wide band like a road connecting up all the circles like this. . ." and he opened a book which he took out of his briefcase and passed it around for us to look at. It was a coloured aerial photograph and it was absolutely clear and unmistakable.

"Have you seen that before, Tim?"

I shook my head, I hadn't, but if the others needed proof of my tunnel underground here was unexpected confirmation. Even if it was solid rock underground now and only showed up as a slight discoloration of crops, it did confirm my memories.

"Look at the time – it's after midnight!" exclaimed Kate.

"Yes, you two have had a tiring day. We ought to split up this party now, I think, and meet again tomorrow." The professor was the decisive chairman again, breaking up his meeting. He was staying at The Golden Lion in Northallerton and volunteered to drop Kate off at her flat, and Bob and Frank were staying with me overnight. For some minutes all was hustle and bustle as the simple administrative facts of everyday existence brought us back from our theorising. We'd arranged to meet in The Golden Lion the next day for lunch, when Professor Stewart would be treating us. It wasn't long before we were in bed, each with our own thoughts of a past greatness disappeared from the earth.

Sleep didn't come easily, but gradually it crept in and erased the conscious memory, but no doubt it had no effect at all on those deep depths of the mind with its fabulous hoards of memory locked away from the everyday mind for some unknown reason.

*

With the coming of the day and ringing of the church bell in the village for morning service, sleep fled away as silently as it had come, leaving me refreshed after the strains of the previous day. We had all slept late, for it was the ten o'clock bell that was ringing. By the time we'd all washed and shaved, and Frank Cooper always took an age shaving, it was time to head for Northallerton and The Golden Lion.

By twelve thirty I'd picked up Kate en route and, parking in front of the hotel, we joined the others in the bar for a pre-lunch drink.

Everyone of course had now had time to think about our discussion of the previous evening, and so the conversation was waged across a new battlefield of theories, although nothing new emerged until we'd begun lunch and had reached the main course of roast beef.

The professor paused in the process of serving up a slice of beef and pointed his knife at me.

"You realise, of course, that all this theorising about earlier societies and fusion reactors and so on is all very interesting, and it all undoubtedly does have a point, but it is tending to divert us from the main path of this research project. How did you, Tim, know all this? Where did you get the knowledge from? How did Kate act as your output device?"

He was, as always, right. We were getting carried away with the past. The professor continued cutting his beef, while the rest of us took our turn to pause.

"Yes, you are right, Professor." Bob had put down his knife and had actually got his fingers into his waistcoat pocket, this time because he'd got his suit on.

"How is Tim able to do this time travelling? Does he actually time travel, or is it something else?"

"I have a theory." The professor informed us in his quiet Scot's burr. He didn't even look up from his plate. We waited for him to go on, which eventually he did.

"Consider what we know of the reproduction of a human being. That is in itself an extremely complex business with masses of data being passed to the new cells at their conception. A human being derives half of its chromosomes from each parent, making up twenty three pairs of chromosomes. Now the chromosomes carry the ultra-microscopic units we call genes, which determine hereditary traits like eye colour, blood group, and all the rest of the master plan which goes to make us up. What if, in addition to doing all we know about, a detailed memory is also transferred?"

"That would be a sort of race memory."

"Yes, Kate, it would contain a miscellany of memories from both your mother and father, and that would build up as massive memory as we go back through the generations. We know that Tim never moved out of the Thornborough Circles physically, but he *did* go back in time. He already had all those memories locked up in some fantastic way inside his head and was able to retrieve them into a part of his mind where they could be broken down and studied."

"Phew. . ." Bob Atwell was staring at the professor.

"That, if you don't mind me saying so, Jim, is a mind-boggling thought. What you are saying in essence is that each of us has a historical capsule of memories going back to. . . to when? Just think of all the interlocking memories we must all have."

"There would have to be some mechanism for only storing the same memory once, otherwise the amount of duplication would be fantastic." Frank Cooper too was treating the suggestion seriously and was already applying his computer storage technique to the horrific, mind-boggling storage problem.

Kate almost seemed to be more practical with her question.

"But, Professor, with our normal genes we inherit some genes from one parent and some from the other, or at least some genes from one or other parents dominate, don't they?" She was obviously very vague about the process as, I must admit, I was too. "What effect would a similar arrangement have on a memory gene?"

"I really have no idea, Kate. If it's true, there is a vast amount of research to be done to understand the technique."

"Do you realise that this would explain quite a lot of things, Tim." It was interesting to see the different people at the table grappling with this new idea, trying it on for size and coming up with their own conclusions. No one had rejected the idea at all and now Bob Atwell, his lunch forgotten, had another angle. . . "It would explain things like reincarnation. You know the sort of thing I mean. You hear about these people being hypnotised and relating things about an apparently previous experience."

"Yes, it would explain that because when I remembered about the control room in the tunnel I felt it was me, but if what the professor theorises is true, then it was one of my ancestors and he has passed that particular memory on."

"We've been very lucky picking Thornborough and you having an ancestor who was there as well, Tim."

Frank had hit on an interesting point which Kate then went on to amplify. "That would explain why when Tim cast around for later memories of the circles, he couldn't find any. Only that particular point in time did he have any association with the circles."

"It explains the Roman Soldier as well, at Housesteads, doesn't it? I wonder how many more places I could go to and find I had some previous knowledge of them too," I wondered half to myself. None of us wanted a sweet with our lunch now, but we settled for coffee.

"So, Professor, is that the end of the mystery of the brain? Is all the unknown part of it really there to deal with this vast log of historical information? Is our future to sort out how to get to it as a matter of course? Is there some relatively easy process which everyone can use?"

For a while, the professor, who was facing the window onto the High Street, sat without answering. He stared out of the window. No one else volunteered an answer. The professor had taken his thick glasses off and his eyes were not focused on anything at all. Perhaps his brain was having its vision of the future. What couldn't the human race achieve with such a tantalising pool of experience? But no, Professor Stewart might have had that sort of vision, but he wasn't entirely satisfied with it as a total explanation. Eventually his eyes came into focus and he put on his glasses again. I never could understand where he got all his paper clips from. I'm sure he must have carried a supply in his pocket.

"No, Tim, I'm sure there's more than that. Even with all that memory that knowledge would give us, it isn't another road for mankind. It's the same road. It would be wider and it would stretch back further, but it wouldn't be a new road. Call it premonition if you like, but I feel it in my bones that there is something else in this thing, something that will one day change man."

"Are you starting to have these mental changes like Tim, Professor?" Frank asked, a little worried.

"No, Frank, what we've managed to forget is that we already know something else exists."

Bob clicked his fingers. "Of course. . . Kate."

We all looked at her.

"Yes, Kate," confirmed the professor. "We might conceivably have part of the answer to Tim's strange experiences, but what about Kate? How does she merge with Tim's mind? No, Tim, there's something else. Before we all settle down to a detailed experimentation of this historical phenomena I think we have to try out one or two more experiments."

"Okay," I agreed with him. "I'm game. What's next on your programme? It sounds like you've got it all worked out."

"Tim, I want to go back to the Thornborough Circles today." Kate had spoken while the professor was drawing breath to reply. She'd now stopped him answering because this wasn't in his plan at all.

"Why, Kate?" I asked her for all of us.

"Well, we know it's an easy place for us to experience this withdrawal into the inner mind – by the way, we ought to give the process a name sometimes, oughtn't we?"

"Yes, that's a good idea," agreed, Bob, allowing himself to be side-tracked from the main point by Kate. "What about something to do with the memory. Think of—"

"No!" Professor Stewart was very emphatic. "I've already said that it might have a much wider application than memory. We won't name it yet." It wasn't a suggestion, the professor was making a simple dogmatic statement which no one was going to oppose, least of all Kate. She was a little taken aback, but undaunted she continued.

"Oh. . . well. . . As I was saying, I think it's time we made a point of trying to get Tim to communicate with me directly, instead of only me being able to communicate with him. If I can do it, he can. He only has to look around and find the mechanism. So far, he's been too concerned casting around generally. Let's do some specific work."

"But today, Kate?"

"Why not? We're all in the mood. It's still only half past two. We can be there within half an hour. There are still a couple of hours of daylight left."

I was suddenly aware that everyone was looking at me. The idea obviously appealed to them, and I must say it appealed to me too.

*

By half past three we were parked on the grass verge by the opening into the field, leading to the centre Thornborough Circle. Logic had told me that the professor was right when he said that there must be something else. But as I crossed the field towards the rise of the circle, I was suddenly very confident that there *was* something else. It was a powerful fact that this site and Fountains and Rievaulx, and no doubt countless others, acted as resonant sites having an effect on the brain. An inexplicable effect which couldn't be put down totally to memory.

We entered the circle and Kate and I stood as we'd done the previous afternoon. Well wrapped up against the cold breeze that eddied around inside the circle looking around for the way out, we looked into each other's eyes, but this time I didn't close them. Grey to grey, we stared into each other's depths and concentrated. I relaxed my muscles and felt the now familiar wave of mental energy soar into my brain. The grey curtain flashed aside and Kate was communicating with me. I had been about to plunge into the vast storage areas again, but Kate called. Silently her mind reached across the gap between us, now very clear and incisive. She held my communications network very effectively and reached out laterally along the channel searching. I knew that I could have stopped her if I'd wanted, but it was very important that I didn't. Lateral searching on this particular level didn't throw up memories, but it showed me new highways waiting for connection. Most looked to be memory highways, but it became clear that some of them contained the necessary information to do different operations. But Kate knew what she was looking for. In many ways it was a search similar to the memory of the tunnel beneath the Thornborough Circles, because there were masses of material whose use was completely unknown. From my conscious mind came an echo of Professor Stewart propounding his theory about memory genes. Here was evidence that he was absolutely right, but at the same time, at this level of brain activity I knew that he was only just touching the truth of the matter.

Kate was transmitting excitement in a powerful surge that very nearly overwhelmed me. She put out her hands to steady me and I gripped them tightly with mine. I looked deeper and deeper into her eyes. I realised that I had conscious control of the everyday level of understanding at this present communications lower level. At the same time as I realised that, I realised that I could control this mental mechanism that Kate had discovered. Hesitantly, I made contact with my main communications channel. I staggered again, this time under the mental impact of thought waves all around me. I could feel them in the air. I recovered and manipulated the digital system and the cacophony faded. Careful now, a little gentle tuning and I had Kate stronger than ever. I had her on my own external communications channel. Even at this point I hesitated before reaching out with this new communications wave. Alpha waves and beta waves, etc. we'd known about, but these waves ,whatever their future designation – perhaps K waves – were going to change completely and forever the relationship between Kate and myself. I reached out and felt her response. I barely had to ask for access. There was certainly a barrier to contact there if she had wanted to use it, but she didn't. I have no words to describe the consequent joining of minds that took place. Many people achieve at the purely physical communications level a oneness, a feeling of love, a feeling of belonging to each other, which is virtually indescribable, but we surpassed this. In parallel with the fusion of our minds we fell into each other's arms with our physical bodies.

For minutes (or was it hours?) we were lost in each other. Across the ages man had reached out for companionship with other human beings, but in this coupling of the minds, companionship and love was taken to a higher level by a whole order of magnitude. Were we with the gods? Who knows? At that point in time we felt we were. With some reluctance we agreed to return to the world in the field of the circle. But before returning I used the same technique that I'd used previously. I concentrated a data block of information from the last few minutes and passed it to my everyday brain, or really to what was more and more evidently the central processor of a vast complicated communications network. It was similar in many ways to the central processor of a computer system which had its own limited storage capability, but once possession of an efficient communications system and some means of mass storage of programs and data it became fantastically powerful.

I followed the data package and felt the bodily warmth of Kate, as I retrieved the sense from my motor senses. We immediately became aware of our three friends in the neighbourhood, looking anxiously on. We released each other and I could easily remember the warmth of our feeling for each other. There was no way that we could ever be separated now.

"Are you both okay?" The professor still took the polite question first, but he rapidly followed it up with a question on what had happened.

We pleaded time to sort it out, while we drove back to my cottage where we were faced with an impatient trio wanting to know our results.

This time I was able to explain them myself. I was now confident that in any future experiment I would be able to remember what had taken place and I said so.

"You think that you've cracked this projection of information upwards to the brain, then, Tim?" Bob was fascinated.

"I do, yes. In fact, if next time I was to look around, I'm sure that I'd find the recent memories of what happened at the Abbeys and Housestends and Thornborough and I'll be able to bring them into my conscious mind."

"Tim, if you can do that, you could write it all down. That would be a big advance in itself. So far we've relied on Kate. Useful as that has been, a first-hand account just must be so much better."

"Okay, well, I suppose we have to call it a day for this weekend and go back to work tomorrow. Can we meet again next week, Professor?"

"I'm sorry, I can't get here next week. It's going to have to be in a fortnight's time. But I hope that you can all make it then. I think the input of ideas from people of different backgrounds is good. It's helping no end."

Bob and Frank had reached a stage now where they were so involved that wild horses wouldn't drag them away from this investigation. It was a case of them being offended now if we wanted to keep them out, which of course we didn't.

It was, however, a measure of how this thing had pulled us all so tightly together.

As everyone was preparing to go, I looked at Kate and she nodded without a word.

"Oh, before you all leave I would like you all to come to our wedding." I held out my hand to Kate and she took it tightly. This was the only physical solution to our mental meeting, and we'd decided this before we left the Thornborough Circles.

Amidst all the exclamations of surprise and congratulations, there was one face that held no surprise. I knew that Jim Stewart knew how and why it had happened. He was last to leave and he clasped both of our hands and said nothing. He only smiled, a sad smile I thought, as he waved goodbye.

Chapter Thirteen
Joined in Mind

We had promised Professor Stewart that we wouldn't try to delve into my subconscious until he was there, and that wasn't going to be until the last weekend in February. He wasn't at all sure what the next step in the chain was to be so he arranged to come and stay with me from the Friday evening to give us time to do some planning.

In the meantime we didn't find his embargo in the least arduous. We had plenty to do. After all, once we'd decided to get married there was going to be no long period before the service. We decided on March 11th, and not entirely surprisingly we decided that the place to get married in was Northallerton Church. The fortnight was very easily taken up with making arrangements. The weekend in between was fully occupied. On the Saturday we raced off to Sheffield to see Kate's parents and on the Sunday into Teesside to see mine. I'm afraid that it was a bit of a shock for both sets of parents because neither of them had the least inkling that we d even met each other, let alone were going to get married. On the whole they absorbed the impact well, but it was obvious that neither of them could understand just why we wanted to get married so quickly. But at the same time it must have been patently obvious to them that we were so sure of each other, for there was no argument after the initial surprise. None of the parents was told about the strange events of the past three months or so. We weren't intending to have a very big wedding, but it was getting quite a size anyway towards the end of the fortnight.

When Friday evening arrived and I picked Kate up at school to take her to the cottage to meet the professor, we were both looking forward to Saturday for it would mean that we could be close again for some precious time. Kate practised being a housewife and prepared dinner for eight o'clock when we expected Professor Stewart to arrive. He was pretty close to time considering the distance he'd travelled. It was the first time that we'd sat down for a dinner together other than in a hotel, and Kate insisted on serving it herself. We had an undeclared truce on the subject matter while we had an excellent meal of home-made soup, stuffed fillet of pork washed down with a medium dry hock, and this time we completed the meal with a sweet, a sort of chocolate meringue with masses of cream. Surprisingly, the professor made quite a pig of himself over this, and I must admit to being not far behind him. It wasn't until we'd returned to the lounge and had coffee poured into our cups and a good Spanish brandy in our glasses that we broke the truce.

We savoured the stillness, the peace of mind and body engendered by a good meal, but finally Kate couldn't stand it any longer.

"Professor, you've had two weeks to consider the next step. Where is it to be and what is it to be? Can we get down to a detailed examination of Tim's ancestors?" She'd said that just a little too glibly with the merest push in the direction that she would like to see the venture move – the safe direction into the past – but the professor was not to be so easily diverted.

"Kate, do you really believe that that's what you and Tim want to do – to look back over your shoulders. Isn't that being a little less than adventurous?"

Kate coloured and had a slightly sheepish look. "But it's the safe way. . ." She soldiered on, fighting a battle she already knew was lost.

"All right, Kate, if that's what you really want to do, we'll do it and spend the next 'n' years of weekends cataloguing history. Very valuable, yes undoubtedly, and no doubt we'll make some strange and exciting finds, but is that the mainstream? Shouldn't we be looking to the future? Is the whole of that mass of brain power bound up with historical record? I don't think so, Kate, and Tim doesn't. . . and you don't, Kate."

"But, Professor, you don't *know* that, do you?"

"Yes, we do Kate. . ." I broke in, taking hold of her hand.

"Remember all those communication channels we saw two weeks ago when we were looking for the means of communicating fully together. Even the secrets of man's survival, and we have to investigate them, you know – we can't ignore them, can we? Can we?" I repeated with some emphasis to an unhappy Kate.

Her grey eyes were filled with tears as she replied almost in a whisper. "No, Tim, we can't ignore them. . . unfortunately."

The professor was obviously upset by Kate's attitude, but although he had sympathy with it he was questing for the greatest thing in his career. He didn't know what it was, but already he'd had a glimpse of Aladdin's Cave and he needed me to go on to show him the way.

For the moment he didn't push for direct action, he took a different line. "You know, Kate, I've been thinking in the last couple of weeks and I think that Tim and yourself aren't the first people with this gift. There are legends throughout history of strange mystics. One of the most famous is Merlin, the wizard from King Arthur's round table. Is he just legend or was he a real person, like you and me? I believe he was, but with his powers he was born into the wrong age. The world hadn't evolved sufficiently to understand him. So through the ages there have been other individuals with the gift. Tim's gift."

"But has the world evolved far enough yet, Professor? Is it ready for Tim's gift, as you call it, or will it ostracise him or worse?"

"Unfortunately, Kate, we can only find that out by going on and on testing the world."

"*If* we do go on. . .?" The professor raised a quizzical bushy eyebrow at me.

". . .okay, *when* we go on. At what point do we make our findings public?"

"I've thought about that too, Tim. The ordinary world could be very dangerous for you once this gets out. . ." He cast a quick glance at Kate, because he knew well enough that her fears had not been directed at the real known world, but at the unknown world.

". . .I've also had some advice from my friend in the Ministry, who has advised us to keep it all under wraps for now, until the extent of this power is known."

"Do you have any concept of the extent of the power, Professor?"

"No, Kate, I have no answers yet, but there are several obvious avenues to try at the moment."

"Which are?" I urged him closer to a decision.

"Well, one thing stands out to me. You remember when Tim finished up in hospital? He didn't just collapse, he was flung back, and that just had to have something to do with his mind power."

"No, Professor, not that. Not until after we're married anyway."

"But don't you see? There's a strong chance that Tim has the power to move himself simply by extracting power from somewhere and directing it. Don't you see the tremendous potential in that?"

"Yes, I do, and I see a tremendous danger too. That definitely will have to wait until after the wedding."

Intentionally or not, the professor had jolted Kate out of her moments of irrational weakness. No, that wasn't fair – it wasn't irrational weakness. Perhaps she could visualise the future better than any of us. She was quite determined now, though. She was a woman, determined not to have her wedding disrupted. The professor capitulated under the verbal attack.

"Right, Kate, but there's another path we can take this weekend if you're willing."

"What is it?"

"It's really you, Kate. Let's do for you what you did for Tim two weeks ago."

"Do you mean, show me the way to—"

"Yes. I would think that now you two can 'talk' fully. I use the word 'talk' very loosely of course. Tim can show you how to open up your sub-mind area."

Kate was obviously attracted by this idea, and I must admit that it appealed strongly to me too. I hadn't thought of it before but if anything was to happen to me, if Kate could do it, then everything wouldn't be lost. The professor was looking after his science, but nevertheless the idea might have a personal bonus too in letting Kate and myself come even closer together.

"Yes, I agree." Kate was fully recovered. "Are we going back to Thornborough again?"

"For the moment yes, but possibly for the last time for a while. I think we ought to try some other places to confirm our ideas."

"Right, that's settled then. We go to the Thornborough Circles tomorrow. That should keep us going until the wedding."

"Ah yes, the wedding!"

I detected an undertone in the professor's comment. I waited, for he obviously hadn't finished. Like magic, a paper clip had appeared in his fingers and was about to undergo a transformation into an unpremeditated shape.

"Thank you for the invitation, but I notice that it's to be at Northallarton Church. I thought you were a Catholic, Tim. Shouldn't you be getting married at a Catholic church?"

"I'm sorry we're going against your fixed views on these things, Jim—"

He held up a hand, stopping me before I worked up to a full-scale defence.

"Don't get me wrong, Tim. I don't have fixed views on this. I was only interested to know why you had taken this particular path to matrimony."

"To tell you the truth, Professor, there was never any question. There was no decision to be taken. Neither of us contemplated any other place. It's where we really started on the road to finding each other."

"Wasn't that at Fountains Abbey or Rievaulx?"

"True, but Northallerton is the first practical place for a marriage."

"And what of God, Tim. Does he come into the wedding?"

I had to think deeply about this question. It was really the main question behind the professor's probing on the point and it wasn't the conventional question of what was God or did I believe in him. The whole question was deeper than that.

"It's funny that you should ask that question, Jim – Kate asked a very similar one some weeks ago."

"And what did you say to her?"

So I gave him my theory about scaffolding surrounding a central truth and it not mattering too much what the scaffolding was or what shape it took, but I emphasised the need for it to maintain the central truth through the years.

"And so I ask again, Tim, after all you've been through in the last months, does God still come into this wedding? Is he still waiting in Northallerton Church for you in two weeks time?"

"He is, Professor, yes." Kate had suddenly answered for me very positively.

"Yes, I agree with Kate. He will be there. Amidst all the scaffolding of the church service, of the ceremony, he will be there trying to communicate."

"Ah... Is the use of that word significant? Can God communicate with you or me, Tim, or are we just so much dirt as far as he is concerned?"

"We could be, I suppose, but I don't think so. He is watching us, waiting, just waiting for us to communicate with him."

"Don't you mean waiting for us to pray to him, Tim?"

"Isn't it the same thing, Professor? Prayer, communication?"

"But, Tim, little over two weeks ago you couldn't communicate with Kate, other than in what is now a very second-rate way between you. Is the human race going to improve its communications with God? If it can, it might have a much greater destiny."

I suddenly could see his drift. The human brain was a vast communications network. I had already proved that. Did it have the ability of communicating directly with something else – the thing we called God? The idea was frightening.

Kate then went on to complicate things further. She'd also followed the drift of the questioning and went on to push it a little further. "You and Tim are talking about Tim, or anyone with the ability, communicating with God, whatever he is, via some supercommunications channel in the sub-brain. So you are starting to term 'the brain' as a receiver, a transmitter, and a processor of information. The brain, however, is commonly regarded somewhat differently. It is thought to be the home of the spirit that is you, Tim Drummond, or you Professor Stewart. Is it, Tim? If we dig around in those depths of your brain, will we find some special place that is reserved for you? Are you in there somewhere? Will I eventually find you, and you, me? Or is this you-ness a spirit or a wraith temporarily held, diffused throughout the body that is yours?"

I wasn't able to answer her, nor was the professor. We were into deep water now and the professor threw in another bucketful!

"Which leads us to ask further of God. If he is waiting for you in Northallerton Church, what is he? Is he too a sort of superbrain or communications system able to communicate with all types of beings and plants and matter and radiate energy and order? Could we, the essential we, that is, be all part of this God?"

This was a new view of God, which wasn't too different from my own concept. In fact, it fitted reasonably well into the scheme of things, but no doubt would be refuted by the official church which nevertheless talked about us all being part of the mystical body of

Christ. Perhaps they only had one word wrong – substitute brain for body!

We followed this trend of discussion up several avenues for an hour or so before we had to tackle the washing up. That mundane tedious task brought us back to earth very effectively, and shortly after that I took Kate back into Northallerton.

Saturday dawned, and Bob Atwell arrived early on the heels of the postman. At the same instant the telephone went. It was Frank Cooper. He couldn't come this weekend as he had to go into work unexpectedly. Bob Atwell too had to be back in Hartlepool by five o'clock! So we decided on an early start and to work through lunchtime. It was almost beginning to feel like a form of work project now, with Professor Stewart as the project manager.

He stage-managed us into the theatre of operations for noon that particular Saturday. The winter was beginning to show signs of dropping its hold on the landscape. I noticed that there were snowdrops near the hedge back on the roadside by the entrance to the field where we stopped our car. As there were only four of us this time we were all in the professor's car. Just as we were about to get out he started the engine again.

"What are you doing, Jim?"

"It's okay, Tim, don't worry. I just thought it might be interesting to take a look at one of the other circles first and perhaps check the effect in a slightly different location."

We drove past the gravel quarries to the T-junction by the river, and turning right drove into West Tanfield only to turn right again back out of the village. This short diversion brought us very quickly by road to the north-western circle. It lay in a wood, just beyond a farmhouse, the trees growing all over the mounds. Just as the road took a sharp bend around the trees there was a place to park on the roadside. Here, there was no gap in the fence and we had to climb over. There were only faint tracks in the undergrowth so it was a bit of a fight to make our way towards the centre of the wood. We made its however, with a bit of scrambling, and there was no doubt that this was a circle; in fact, the trees had preserved the mounds of the circle better than in the other circle in the open field.

The change in location had no effect on my ability to submerge into my subconscious. In fact, if anything it was probably rather

easier, though that was probably more due to practice than anything else.
This time we held both hands and concentrated. For a moment I was held to the everyday by the distant sound of a jet aircraft, probably going in to land at RAF Leeming. Then I fell into the well of the sub-brain and almost in the same instant caught hold of Kate's mind. She was troubled and worried about this adventure into the unknown, despite the fact that she had voyaged into the depths of my mind and knew pretty well the sort of thing she might expect to find there.
Yes, I was in full overlap with Kate's mind, with her central processing area, but there were no other paths open. There appeared to be no other communications channels or connections. Had we stumbled across some big difference between a man and a woman? The communications channel to the outside world was much sharper than mine. Almost I felt that with a little effort on Kate's part she could contact Professor Stewart. I was sure that the ever so faint signal hovering around in the misty peripheral area belonged to him.
I realised that possibly her biggest problem was that she was still holding on to the real world. She wasn't relaxed enough. Almost subconsciously she didn't want to let go. But, as I thought that, she instantly knew what I was thinking and I could feel her respond. She controlled her breathing and her whirling thoughts. Slower, deeper, limit the amount of current information being moved around. Try to establish a blank mind. In the context of what we were doing, to do that was of course impossible, but we had to strive for comparative peace of mind.
Here it was. Or was it? For a fleeting instant I thought I'd detected that beam of sizzling energy, the carrier beam. Like a flash of sheet lightning, it seemed to light up the whole of the central brain area as it came again, unmistakably this time, but diffused throughout the cortex. I could feel the excitement building inside Kate now. She was losing her doubts. She was no longer afraid. She joined me in my search for the opening channel. Where had it come from? A sudden outpouring of burbling uncontrolled energy and it seared forth again – this time like a bolt of lightning. No longer diffuse and virtually undetectable, it had concentrated itself into a central beam of energy, capable of delving like some sub-mini-micro laser beam into the unknown depths and like a laser beam providing thousands of

parallel communications channels for vast amounts of information. Each of these channels was capable of transmitting packages of concentrated information in a form similar to a time division multiplexing system.

For some time this channel wavered and blurred and roared and screamed as Kate fought to control it. This revealed a very interesting point. Much as I wanted to help her, I couldn't. I could communicate and advise, but she had to exert the actual control herself. She had to be able to do this in order to progress. Without the laser-like access channel we couldn't delve into Kate's past history. It flashed and I could see that she was coming to grips with the control but she was tiring rapidly. I don't know how long she battled against this channel of energy which had been unrestrained for so long. Slowly but surely her expertise improved and soon she could switch it on and off at will, and then and only then did we set out on a mental exploration. I realised that Kate was very tired now, and my own experience indicated that when I was tired through exerting a lot of energy, I couldn't hold on to the ability to penetrate into the ever-denser layers of neurons.

We only had time for a quick scout around the information banks picking up general characteristics rather than details, and it looked very similar to my own. The historical data went back in much the same way as mine with much of the same general information to be found, but the detail differed of course. She was failing now and the channel was roaring and corrupting information.

Before coming back up from the sub-brain areas I had a quick look around my own sections. I ignored the historic information files and began to search for something else. Immediately Kate recognised what I was doing and I was overpowered by a fantastically-powered transmission, which in essence shouted 'No' across the ethereal wave band. Kate was so close physically, and I'd had no resistance in my reception of her that this increase in power completely obliterated my search pattern and forced me to rocket out of the well of sub-knowledge in order to got a grip on all the everyday brain actions like the motor devices of breathing, standing etc.. The level of interference had been so great that it was causing an imminent collapse of all communications.

As far as Kate was concerned, it had the desired effect. She forced me along with her into the conscious world just at the point in time that I was collapsing. As we had been holding hands together Kate gave me support, so the final result was a stagger rather than a collapse, but I had one hell of a headache. As a last effort I had fortunately remembered to transfer the current packet of information from the background brain to the everyday storage, so I was able to remember what had happened and was able to give Professor Stewart a rather mundane description of Kate's search and subsequent fight to control her new-found power.

"I'm sorry, Professor, that the description is so poor. The problem in describing it, I suppose, is akin to describing colour to someone who has been blind from birth. They can have no possible conception of the beauty, of the range of information contained in a glance. I'm afraid that you will just have to accept that the English language, or any other for that matter, has not the words to adequately describe the experiences."

The professor and Bob Atwell had helped us back to the car and we were on our way back to the cottage so that Bob could get back home for the evening. He'd let us recover a little before asking about what had happened. In actual fact he was getting the answers from me this time. The experience had obviously been somewhat overwhelming for Kate and she was dropping off to sleep in the back of the car. I had carefully avoided any mention of why we'd suddenly returned to the current world, but Bob Atwell was very perceptive as usual.

When I'd finished talking, he just looked over his shoulder and looked me straight in the eyes.

"Did you find your communication channel to God, then?" We stared each other out for some moments, but Bob had won this round and it was me who had to drop the challenge.

"No, Bob, I didn't."

His use of the word 'God' was of course deliberately provocative in line with his blunt nature and West Riding manner. But I knew that he meant it as a genuine question and, more to the point, I knew exactly what he was asking about. I hadn't been able to resist searching for a channel of communications to something else which I just knew had to be there somewhere.

I explained then that Kate had known what was happening and had vetoed it.

"But," the professor was quick to notice, "you said that you weren't able to control anything that she was doing. You *did* say that you weren't able to help her other than by making thought suggestions, didn't you? So how could *she* stop you doing what you wanted to do?"

"I agree, Jim, I did say that and it's true too. She wasn't able to control any of my processes in the normal way, but she put out such a harsh strident intercommunication signal that it was the signal which acted an a total interference to my network until I was able to eliminate it. It was particularly more potent as there was no guard at all against it and it was so unexpected."

The professor nodded to himself as be concentrated on driving along the winding road from Busby Stoop to South Otterington, between the A1 and Northallerton.

For the remainder of the journey home we each held our own peace, our own thoughts, and Kate slipped into sleep, a sleep of the exhausted. She had to be woken up when we reached the cottage. She was so tall that we couldn't possibly envisage lifting her out without awakening her. So by the time we got her into the cottage and I'd made a hot cup of coffee for everyone she was in a reasonably intelligent state again.

"Look, Tim, I'm afraid I'm going to have to go home now. I promised Margaret that I'd be home without fail tonight. We're going out for dinner."

"Don't apologise, Bob, just go."

"But what about next week? Have you anything planned?"

I looked at the professor. Before answering, he in turn looked at Kate. "No, Tim, I have no plans for next week. I think that we've got enough information for now to think about and analyse. We've made tremendous progress in the last few weeks and I think at the moment that it is more important for Tim and Kate to finalise their wedding arrangements and get married. We have to look to the future generations, you know – we can't ignore them."

"You mean, you'd like to see what kind of a child they will produce between them?" Perceptive as ever and also blunt as ever, Bob had interpreted the professor's remarks in a particular way which, but for him, I might have missed in all innocence. There was no doubt when I looked at Jim Stewart that that was exactly what he had meant. Beneath his beard he coloured ever so slightly, while at the same time denying that was what he had meant.

"Never mind, Professor." Kate diverted attention from him. "We'll call him after you if you'll be his godfather."

He laughed at that.

"We're all getting a bit in advance of things, aren't we? You've got to got married yet and being a godfather raises all sorts of problems to people who believe that God is just a communications network in the sky."

"I didn't say that, Professor."

He laughed again. "No, Tim, of course you didn't. I was just pulling your leg." But be had nevertheless touched me on what was a sensitive subject just at the moment.

"So, anyway," butted in Bob, "you are going to get married before anything else happens?"

"Yes." Kate was very firm about it.

"Except. . ."

"Except what, Tim Drummond?"

"Well. . ." I tantalised her, drawing out my reply. ". . .I might just start writing down what has happened now that I've been able to recover the memories of what actually did happen."

"That should manage to be a nice confusing document." Bob put in a parting shot. "We've been mightily confused most of the time, and if you are trying to write about the present and the past combined, it might well prove impossible. Anyway, the best of luck with it, Tim. Cheerio for now."

And Bob disappeared, leaving us to the remainder of the weekend, the weekend before the wedding.

Chapter Fourteen
Northallerton Church

And so I began to write this description of my mental journeyings in order that if anything should happen to me at least there was a main outline of the events and our thoughts about them and our actions at those points in time.

I continued at work during that week before the wedding until the Thursday. I was in fact only taking a week and a day off work because we were coming up close to the commissioning of our new chemical plant. In fact, on the Monday of that week we concluded two years of argument and nerve fraying over the plant computer system. After an initial rejection of the system during acceptance trials eighteen months earlier, we had had a continual running battle with both the main contractor and the computer supplier. This had, of course, had a loading effect on the minds of those involved. This worrying effect had increased in the last few months and weeks as the computer first of all approached and then came onto the critical path. In this last week we recommenced acceptance trials under great pressure, knowing that if we failed again there was no time left, and a new failure would mean delaying a multi-million pound chemical plant. This time, however, it had sailed through the tests much to many people's amazement, and there was a tremendous sense of anticlimax in my section. The bitter hassle of the past months continued to the bitter end, even through the meeting, convened to sign the acceptance certificates for the installation, and what should have been a quarter of an hour meeting, lasted for two hours. But all things have to come to an end sometime, and eventually the certificates were signed with three signatures – one from each of the companies concerned. I have related this information because it was important to realise that this work had imposed an unknown strain on my mind which was suddenly released on the Monday before our wedding.

That evening Kate came to the cottage to make some final, organisational arrangements for the wedding, and by about ten o'clock we'd had enough.

"Come on, Kate, let's have a walk."

"At this time of night?"

"Yes, a quick walk up the village and back will clear our heads before you go home for the night."

She thought about it for a few moments before, with a sigh, dumping all her lists and papers onto the floor.

"Okay, Tim, but we'll never sort it out, you know."

"Don't worry about it, Kate. Saturday will come and go whatever happens, so go and get your coat."

We locked the door behind us, leaving the porch light on to illuminate our return, and walked down the drive to the gate. It was a perfectly still night with a bright almost full moon, the sky crisscrossed with pinpoints of light.

We paused at the gate, holding hands and wordlessly deciding which way to turn. We turned to the left in the silence, up the village. In the moonlight the village had a ghostly ethereal quality. The moon itself had a massive faint halo, which I'd only rarely seen before. As we walked up the village past its home-made patchwork quilt of gardens and assorted styles of houses, the village worked its magic on me again. This was why I lived in the country, miles away from the hustle and bustle of the Teesside in which I worked. In stark contrast to the smoke and ever-present hum of industry, the yellow street lights diffusing their reflected glare into a dome of luminescence over the town, and its rows and rows of congested houses on postage stamp gardens, here was a stillness. The great centuries-old trees, stark against the night sky, stood quietly on guard over the village and its inhabitants. Tonight they weren't crashing and threshing in their continuous battle against the wind, they were silent and friendly guardians of the peace. The long gardens preparing for spring presented the many housing styles to their best advantage in the moonlight, From Georgian styles to modern styles, and in white concrete, they formed up on each side of us as a guard of honour for our walk. The unobtrusive footpath lights tacked onto the top of the telegraph poles against those nights when the moon failed to shine were not needed tonight, and indeed as we passed the public house and the old village school we noticed that the lights in the upper half of the village were not on at all. But it didn't matter – the moon tonight was all-pervading. We reached the vicarage corner where the children of the village waited for the school bus each morning. I went to turn around the corner, but for the first time Kate spoke.

"No, Tim, not that way, let's go up the bank to the top."

There was no need for a reply. I just followed the direction of her tug, and in another ten minutes we were at the top of Thirsk Bank out of the village. We stopped at the seat near the village name sign and leaned on the fence, looking to the west.

From this point on a nice day you could see for miles across the rich Vale of York to the Pennine range in the distance. Tonight, of course, it was all dark except for the many points of light from farmhouse windows and the blotches of yellow marking Bedale and Richmond, and there, about four miles away, a long snake-like chain of lights racing across the countryside. In reality it was a London-to-Edinburgh train racing its way north on the main railway line. On this still night, that was the only sound to intrude on the magic, and even that eventually faded into the distance to be followed by a series of lights, winking to red and then changing back again first to amber and then back to green. The line was ready for the next package of humanity on their journey north.

Around us in the grass, the daffodils planted by the parish council on the approach to the village were silently pushing their way into prominence ready to burst forth in the not-too-distant future into a riot of yellow colouring. There was not a single cloud in the sky and all the constellations could be clearly identified. I searched the heavens and found The Plough, and thence from the pointers I located the Pole Star.

When we look at the stars we are looking back deep into the past, for we see them, not as they are now, but as they *were* hundreds and thousands of years ago. Light from the sun, takes eight minutes to reach the earth, and from our nearest star, Proxima Centauri, it takes more than four years. From some of the stars of the Milky Way it takes light thousands of years to reach us, so in many ways the star-studded universe is another vast store of history. The ancient Greeks had given many of the constellations their names and they were all bound up with their religious beliefs. As I found the Pole Star in the stillness of this Yorkshire night, I could well understand their fascination with the sky. I could almost feel the great God of the heavens, Zeus, calling. From Mount Olympus he ruled the stars until he became merely a legend, a Greek myth. But was he? Did he really still sit out there, riding the Milky Way, waiting for men to communicate with him again? In the space of time it takes to blink I was out of myself, if not out with the stars I was at least with the artificial satellites which traced their paths in a continuous ring through the heavens. I reached for the stars, leaving my body in Kate's charge for that merest blink of time. I was outside myself looking back to the little village, set under the hillside, the two human figures leaning close together against the fence above the village.

Then I felt the fence hard under my hand again and Kate warm and close beside me. I'd been dreaming of course. Or had I, my mind totally relaxed for the first time in the months that I had learnt meditation? It had learnt new things about itself – how to drive into its own depths and communicate in wonderful mystic ways with another human mind. Was there still something new here that it could do? Again I let the peace and stillness of the night wash into me and through me. As I gazed into the heavens and found the Pole Star again, the star around which all the heavens wheeled and rolled.

At one with them for a moment, it happened again – that strange blink in time and space when I felt I could gather together all the mysteries of the stars, and then it was gone again, as the distant roar of a London-bound train disturbed the stillness for a few minutes.

"Come on, Tim. It's a magic night, I know, but it's time we were getting back. I really will have to get an early night tonight."

I lay in bed after she'd gone. Had I imagined it or had it been real? Had I really found, for however fleeting an instant, a way to the stars? I hadn't mentioned it to Kate because I didn't want to worry her before the wedding, but I had no such qualms about telling Bob Atwell.

On the Tuesday, it was lunchtime before I saw Bob. He put his head round my office door on the dot of twelve noon.

"Are you coming, sunshine?" he asked, obviously in a cheery mood.

It was one of those days when there were not many people in the dining-room and we had the table to ourselves so I was able to describe in some detail what had happened, or what I thought had happened the previous evening. He listened and heard me out with that little smile on his face. If you didn't know him, you might well think that he didn't believe a word you were saying. But knowing him, he was thinking deeply about it, taking it all in, and would quickly come out with a judgement. I was right.

"Hey, Tim, that's fantastic. You've found another dimension of thought, haven't you?"

"But have I? How can you call it thought when you move outside of your physical brain, Bob? Remember what we were saying only the other evening about the brain and the essence that is you."

"That could be it, Tim. You could have found the you bit. It could be that which is moving outside the human brain."

"I'm not so sure, though, Bob. It could be that I was able to tap into some other source of transmissions which I was able to interpret as though it was there itself."

"Umm," was Bob's comment on the alternative for the time being.

"You know, Tim," he waved a chip at me, which he shouldn't have been eating at all, according to his diet, "you said something that makes me think. You said that everything you look at in the sky is out of date, some of it by minutes, some of it by years, and it's out of date because it is limited by the speed of light. The speed of light has always been regarded as the ultimate reference. Nothing, but nothing, goes faster. Light is part of the electro-magnetic spectrum of radiated waves. Some of those oscillate at high frequencies and hop across the universe in tiny strides, others vibrate at very low frequencies and travel the universe in simple strides of millions of miles. In those variations the waves still travel the universe at the speed of light, but some of the mechanisms operating in that transmission, which, let's face it, no one really understands yet, must operate faster than light. So maybe it *is* possible to travel faster than light. God knows what possibilities that would create. It just occurred to me, you could have picked up a faster-than-light transmission of yourself. . . No? I'll get some coffee while you think about it."

He got the coffee and sat down again.

"Well, have I convinced you?"

I shook my head. "No. . . but it's an interesting theme to follow, isn't it? Look at the universe again, Bob. As you've said, everything we see there is totally out of date. In a very real sense the universe is a gigantic memory of itself. Everything that's ever happened or is going to happen is or will be stored there as a memory, a light wave travelling at the speed of light. If you could travel faster than light, you'd be able to look back and see yourself travelling – so seeing into the future. Looking at the universe from its *own* point of view rather than yours or mine, time is arguably always now. All time is now. So to tune to the past or to tune to the future, all that is required is some kind of instrument to decode and interpret the information which is travelling around this memory at the speed of light."

"Phew, Tim." It was Bob's turn to shake his head. "You're really getting theoretical there, old son. Are you then suggesting that part of the brain's powers is to decode this type of information?"

"Yes, I am. It all fits into the overall pattern of information that we've been discovering, doesn't it? It pulls people like prophets into the net and explains them away as people who could manipulate their brains – another group of people who in the past used their brain size to good use."

"I must say, Tim, that the idea appeals to me. Just think, if this power could be developed in the future, or now, or in the past perhaps, we did, or can, or will travel in the corridors of time!"

We subsided into silence. There were no words to talk about the ideas we were wrestling with. Once again, we felt the frustration of the limiting power of words. Bob, I was beginning to realise, was even more frustrated than me because, of course, I had the power to lose myself in the depths of my brain. He wasn't able to do that and I couldn't adequately describe what happened for him. But, practical as ever, he came up with a practical problem that this possible information explosion could cause.

"I'm starting to get worried about your brain, Tim. . ."

"You mean, you think I'm going round the bend?" I laughed.

"No." He was not laughing, he was very serious.

". . .I didn't mean that at all, but the part of the brain that we all know and all use must have and does have storage limits. By what you say, in order to remember what you've been doing in your subconscious state, you have to put an informative package together and send it via a switching system to a conscious storage area. Isn't that right?"

"Well, nearly. It's about right insofar as I can explain what happens."

"Right, well, if you continue to do this and try to store all the information you are retrieving and deal with all these communication networks via your conscious brain, you'll overload it, and then what will happen?"

"Probably something very like what happens to a computer, which computes meaningless garbage and crashes."

"Exactly. In other words, you'll go mad."

"Yes. Thank you, Bob. You are a proper Job's comforter, aren't you?" He only pulled a face and shrugged his shoulders. He knew as well as me that while I might make light of it and joke about it, he did have a point. A very serious point.

We walked back over to the offices in a sombre mood. There had to be some solution to this one too somewhere.

I had to go onto the site that afternoon to check that computer information was being entered to the agreed program. After I'd finished the technical discussions I stood in the centre of the new control room with its three main panel sections covered with switches, coloured lights, visual display screens, flashing plant information and alarms. The computer was dealing with all this action via its central processor. An output writer started to chatter quietly to itself at the end of the panel, and I walked over to look at what it was doing. It was rapidly printing and spewing out the shift log, all the historical information of product flows and usages and mass balances during the previous shift. The computer collected all this information and passed it in blocks of information to the discs to be called back into the main memory as and when required.

'As and when required' - the words stuck in my head and looped around and around. 'As and when required'. To be able to cope with the volumes of information in the sub-brain, it had to be accessible as and when required. I had to be able to search for it, bring it forward and return it at will. If I couldn't do that, I'd go mad. My brain, as Bob said, would at some point in time cease to cope. It would become scrambled.

The shift log had mesmerised me. As the printing head raced back and forth across the paper, I realised that I was only halfway to solving the brain riddle after all. Somehow, I had to be able to communicate with my sub-brain at will. I had to reach a stage where I didn't have to stand in the circle at Thornborough or the Priory at Mount Grace to achieve this communication, where I didn't have to lose control of my current everyday level of thought and action. I must be able to manipulate the two areas of my mind at will, as the computer did, giving due priority to the action which needed it the most at any particular instant. More important, I had to be able to return the blocks of information to the sub-brain in the certainty that I would find them again as and when required.

"What's wrong, Tim?" One of my engineers was shaking my arm. "Are you okay?" I realised that the log was finished and the printer still. I'd been staring fixedly at it for some time. I shook my head as though to clear it.

"Yes, John, thanks. I was just thinking." He accepted that but with an odd look at me.

For the remainder of the week Bob and I discussed this need, but we didn't come up with any suggestion as to how it could be achieved. In the meantime, preparations for the wedding were going on and I was continuing to write this account. All the preparations finally came to a head on the Saturday morning. In the normal course of events it would have been sufficient for me to have mentioned the wedding in this account and then passed on to other things. But other things happened at the wedding which makes it a necessary and integral part of this account.

The Saturday morning, as I've said, finally arrived. Not quite a spring morning as it was only the 11th of March, but as I looked from my bedroom window before breakfast I thought that it looked as though the day was doing its best to be a spring day. The sun was climbing into the sky. Although it wasn't a cloudless day by any means, the sun was doing its best to avoid the clouds and on the whole was succeeding quite well.

My stag night at the village pub had been Thursday night, not Friday night, and so I'd had time to recover. My brother was to be best man and he and his wife had travelled across from Cumbria, where they lived, on the Friday. From my point of view the lead-up to the ceremony went well and on time. The taxi from Northallerton arrived and found us without too much difficulty, and we arrived at the church in plenty of time. The town was wearing its usual friendly Saturday morning cloak of market and bustle. It wasn't the hurly-burly bustle of the Teesside towns, it was steadier in Northallerton. Somehow, the pace of life was slower and pleasanter. People had time to stop and chat in the middle of buying their vegetables for the weekend. Shopping wasn't the be-all and end-all of their existence – they had time for other people, not a nosiness, though a towns-person might call it that. It was more a genuine interest in other people.

I could sense the atmosphere of the day as we walked through the churchyard to the church. For a few minutes we stood at the back of the church, talking to those guests who had already arrived. We then decided that it was time to take our places in the front row. As I knelt for a few moments, I remembered the last time I'd been here when Kate's face had been transmitted to me apparently in the halo of an altar candle. I looked to the altar and the candles were there. Today, however, they were having a fight to be seen in the sunlight, which filtered down in long golden shafts of happiness to join the candles in their little dance of joy.

I remained kneeling as the sound of the church clock boomed out over Northallerton town, proclaiming to the shoppers that it was now eleven o'clock.

As the clock struck I knelt, again my face in my hands. Why I did it, I don't know, but something moved me to it. As I put my hands over my face, I shut out the old church, its altar, and the slanting rays of sunlight. My eyes closed. I had no mental distraction and as previously all that I could see was a series of light and dark multicoloured spots, depending on the pressure I exerted with my hands on my eyelids. I visualised Kate in her taxi, passing through the town centre, a few minutes late as every good bride should be. I suddenly realised that I had a faint if indistinct communication taking place. I opened my eyes for a moment. Yes, I was still in church, my brother seated beside me waiting to produce the traditional ring. I felt the seat back hard beneath my hand. No, I wasn't recessing into my sub-brain. There was no trace of that, but I was being communicated with, or was I? No, it was me trying to communicate with Kate. I felt surprise, double surprise – mine and hers. She was thrown in to a flurry as the taxi came around the roundabout at the end of the High Street and made for the church. Her immediate, almost panic-stricken, reaction to this new phenomena was to refuse the communication.

Then she realised that it was me who was making it and allowed the connection. Once I realised what was happening, I stepped up the power of transmission, and from being a shadowy, misty, unworldly contact we fell into a full brain-merging powerful communication.

What a wedding present! At least in near distance we could be in full intimate merged communication.

As she left the taxi and walked through the churchyard to the church door, it was a strange and wonderful experience to feel her doing it just as I had done some minutes previously. It was like an action replay on the television. As she reached the church door, the organist was given the nod and he began to play our choice for the entrance hymn. We all stood at the first notes and faced the altar. It was an incredibly strange experience, a sort of double life. My own senses were feeding information direct to my brain from my position in the church, and at the same time overlaid on these sensations was a now powerful communication from Kate, which transmitted all that her senses were detecting too. The result was a second view of the church from Kate's viewpoint and I could see myself in the front row waiting for her. That, if anything, was the strangest thing of all. It almost reminded me of the night on Thirsk Bank with my momentary disembodiment into the stars. Too late, I realised that I was fully open to Kate, and she picked up my memory of that moment. She stemmed an inquisitive reaction to it. After all, there was a wedding ceremony to go through. Slowly she came up the aisle and stood next to me as I stepped out into the aisle to meet her. As I turned to look at her, the dual sense detection system was almost overwhelming. At one and the same time I looked at myself through her eyes and also I was looking at a Kate, proudly straight and tall in her long white wedding dress and long golden hair fighting its way out from beneath her veil. It reacted strongly and favourably with the suns rays which chose that particular spot to shine on, with a strengthening intensity. So it seemed to me, anyway. For some moments we looked into each other's grey eyes and eventually turned to face the minister as the first hymn burst out - *The Lord's My Shepherd*. I started to sing, but was held quiet by Kate who wanted me to listen to the words.

"My soul he doth restore again and me to walk doth make." The ancient hymn brought down to earth to a normal human understanding. at least for a few minutes, our God - whatever and wherever he was. *"And in God's house for ever more my dwelling place shall be"*

The organ's power disappeared into the heights of the old roof, as the wordy part of the service began. The final words of the hymn were held in my mind. Was the hymn part of the scaffolding of the church, a wishful thinking on behalf of mankind, or was it part of the central structure, part of God's plan? The responses to the simple questions were hardly necessary for us. We both managed to whisper "I do" for the benefit of the vicar and the congregation, most of whom were not aware of the edge of the known world on which we were all standing. Those who did know were all there in the pews behind us. Professor Stewart had come from Sheffield and was with Bob Atwell and his wife, Margaret, and also Frank Cooper and Eileen and little Gillian. Neither Kate's father, who gave her away quite happily, nor my brother, who produced the ring at the right instant, was aware of the future, ours and theirs, balanced so critically in time. Balanced between a rebirth, an explosion of knowledge undreamt-of across the centuries and the alternative, an eclipse of that knowledge perhaps not for the first time across the years as the people charged with its birth failed to deliver it.

The simple moving ceremony moved to its conclusion with the singing of the hymn *O Perfect Love, All Human Thought Transcending*. And again the closing words echoed around in a repetitive loop in my mind searching for an explanation -

"And to life's day the glorious unknown morrow that dawns upon eternal love and life."

Kate had chosen the hymns, but they were loaded with significance and meaning. The thought crossed my mind as we entered the sacristy for the signing of the marriage lines – had she chosen them or had she been directed? Kate didn't know the answer to that one either, and we silently agreed between us to cease this thought-type communication for the rest of the day's proceedings, or we might not get through the day because the emotional effect was too great.

As the strains of Mendelssohn's *Wedding March* echoed around the church and we walked down the aisle together, I had a sudden thought. Communication with Kate had moved from the subconscious realm to the conscious realm. Perhaps with time the fears that I had about scrambling my mind might yet prove groundless. As we passed by the pew in which Professor Stewart was standing, I mischievously threw out a mental communication to him. Now that the control of that communications centre was under the control of the conscious mind, it seemed a very easy thing to do. I did get something of a shock, however, when I received a very dim and woolly echo back. In the same instant I watched the professor's smile go fixed. Behind his beard and under the white hair he'd heard the call. There was no doubt about it. Ghostly and from a great distance he received a sharp reminder and the assurance that this thing, this ability, was spreading. It wasn't yet quite the avalanche that we had talked about, but even avalanches have small beginnings. Then I was past him and couldn't do it again. As we left the church in the taxi after the photographs had been taken, we left behind a puzzled professor. He wasn't sure. Had he heard what he'd thought he'd heard? Or was it a trick, if not of the light, of the service?

Eventually, when all the food was eaten and all drink drunk, and the speeches completed, Professor Stewart couldn't resist it and he sought me out to ask. When I'd told him of the progressive steps in the church, he was almost ecstatic with joy.

"Go on then, Tim, try it again, please."

To please him I did try, but those magic moments in church had passed and my mind, no doubt clouded with food and drink, couldn't again raise an echo, although I was always aware of Kate's presence. We hadn't tried direct communications again, but there was a sort of tell-tale, a carrier wave between us ready and available for communication at any instant we desired. We had no idea yet whether this would be a function of distance and would disappear the further apart that we were physically. That could easily be tested in due course.

We finally got through the merry-making and the last of the guests left us alone in our cottage by about ten o'clock that night. We had planned to have this first night in the cottage and then to have a few days holiday at a hotel on the west coast of Scotland.

We waved off Kate's mother and father, and walked back up the drive to the cottage, but instead of going in immediately we walked around the back into the back garden. My old cottage had quite a large back garden, with a rose garden and an orchard as well as a vegetable patch and some soft fruit bushes. We walked down the garden path to the five-bar gate at the bottom and breathed in the quiet and calm as we had done on Thirsk Bank at this time a week ago. But now it was the peace of reaction – reaction from the noise and bustle of our wedding day. For me, though, the day's surprises were not yet quite complete. We leaned back against the gate and together looked back up the garden to the cottage whose lights could be seen casting giant shadows in the orchard. I put my arm around Kate and ran my hand up and down her bare arm. I felt it, soft and yielding. I could feel the texture of her skin and then, incredibly, something else. Something seen rather than felt. But then, no, *seen* wasn't the correct word either. Detected was a better word, but the mental effect was like seeing. *I could sense the colour of her arm through my fingers.* I moved my hand onto her blouse and felt the change in colour, to white.

I wasn't imagining things, but it felt like another source of radiation which I'd not noticed before. It was equivalent to colour. As yet, it had no form, but very definitely I could see colour with my hand.

Chapter Fifteen
Iona

Our wedding day had produced a totally unexpected advance in my mental facilities and it had been partially matched by a similar advance in Kate's. We had found that we could communicate at will, but only over a distance of a couple of hundred metres. After that the 'reception' seemed to fade very rapidly. But in addition I had acquired a totally unforeseen facility to 'see' colour with my fingers. This was a power which seemed to be present all the time now and added a new dimension to the sense of touch. It could well have been induced by the heightened perception necessary for thought transmissions. The ability to decode a new set of wavelengths into understandable information had obviously spread into the decoding of sense information from the fingers. The fascinating thought, of course, was what other unexpected side powers would be derived from the discovery of main predicted functions?

Kate had, however, insisted on me keeping to my bargain not to progress with the investigation until after our honeymoon. Sunday morning, therefore, found us heading north. Next to living in North Yorkshire, I would like to live on the west coast of Scotland or one of its islands. I was first introduced to Scotland by a friend at school whose family came from Scotland. He persuaded me to hitchhike there, to visit his relations and then to continue into the Highlands. As it happened, that first day we didn't do much hitching. It was more hiking and night found us at Barnard Castle trying to gain access to the youth hostel instead of being over the border. That was the end of my first walk. The next morning found us both nursing sore feet and blisters, sitting on the steps of the railway station, now long closed, waiting for it to open. We did get to Scotland in the end and did some gentle walking in the Campsi Fells. You might think that the experience would have put me off, but it had the opposite effect.

After that, at least once a year I could be found with or without friends extending my knowledge of the Highlands and islands - Skye, Arran, Mull, and even into the Outer Hebrides on North and South Uist. Of all the islands, I preferred the Isle of Mull most. It had, to my mind, the widest variety of all the islands. It was not too big nor too small. It had mountains and forests, hills and moors, cliffs and beaches, and it had a soft and gentle touch in the air. And so it was to Mull that I wanted to take Kate. I wanted her to fall in love with it as I had done. But she had never been north of the border and was a little wary of the supposed restrictions of staying on an island. The result had been a compromise - a hotel on the Ardnamurchan Peninsular opposite the Isle of Mull. This hotel was more of a rich man's folly than one's usual idea of a hotel. It was built of sandstone, which had to be shipped in from Dumfriesshire by the then Laird of Ardnamurchan in 1900. In 1935 the Chairman of Boots had bought the estate and lived there until 1949 when the castle was sold and the rest of the estate broken up. Now a Trust House Forte hotel, I had come across it a few years ago when I ventured up this long single-tract road for the first time. The road was twisting and tortuous, often dipping wildly to the sea, but frequently bordered by masses of rhododendrons. The castle was set well back from the road and was approached via a long winding drive through large iron gates and beautiful gardens full of shrubs and trees, many of them exotic and rare.

We'd made good time to Glasgow, and the road via Loch Lomond was near deserted, which wasn't surprising for this time of the year. We'd had a fairly mild winter on the whole and the snow only lingered across the mountain tops. The drive across Rannoch Moor was through black driving rain mixed with sleet, but as we came out into the Pass of Glencoe the sun was doing its best to penetrate the rain and mist, causing an unworldly light to diffuse through and reflect back from the thousands of rivulets of water cascading down the mountain sides on each side. The sun strengthened as we drove on into the pass, and to our disappointment the effect disappeared. The weather, however, didn't, and soon it was raining hard again. It was getting on for six o'clock at night by the time we reached the ferry at Corran having crossed the bridge at Ballachulish. At Corran there was still one of the old-highland ferries operating. It was little more than a platform which held six to eight vehicles at a time. In the summertime there were often long queues here, but on this particular Sunday there was no trouble getting on. The problem was more one of whether we should go on at all. The sea was running high and choppy as it raced up Loch Linnhe and it tossed the ferry about like a cork. We viewed the incoming ferry with some unease, but the alternative was a long drive of about forty miles around the loch, and so we took the lesser of the two evils. It really was like a cork swinging from side to side quite frighteningly. In fact we took off our driving safety belts in case we had to make a quick exit from the car and have to swim. Our fears in the end proved to be groundless, however, as we came into the shelter of the slipway and we were able to drive off the turntable. I certainly didn't envy the two ferrymen in their bright orange waterproofs on a day like that. Turning left from the slip put us immediately onto the Ardnamurchan road. Just before Strontian, a road, leading eventually to the Mull ferry at Lochaline branched off, and the main road reduced to a single-width track. We eventually made it to the castle by a quarter past seven, having acted as a shepherding car for a flock of wandering sheep and had something of a problem getting past some equally wandering cattle.

Our room, it turned out, was number seventeen at the top of a fascinating circular stairway. It was a large, well appointed room with a large window, set in the very turret of the castle, the view from which was breathtaking. That first evening, of course, it was rather too late to see anything from the windows, but we contented ourselves with a fabulous meal in the restaurant and a relaxed drink in the panelled bar afterwards.

During the next five days we had the best honeymoon anyone could possibly hope for. While tacitly agreeing not to proceed with any investigations, we did allow ourselves to communicate at the mental level most of the time. We were therefore much closer than any normal couple. We did most of the touristy sort of things. We looked for seals in the bay by the hotel. It might have been the wrong time of the year, but we didn't see any. We walked down to the bay called Camus-nan-Geall, where St Columba landed from Iona, and examined the now all-but-disappeared burial ground belonging to the Clan Campbell, and splashed around in our wellington boots in the stream looking for sapphire stones, which it was reputed could be found there. Our luck wasn't in here either as there had been too many other visitors doing the same thing. We stood on the catwalk on the lighthouse at Ardnamurchan Point, the most westerly point of the British mainland, and hung on tightly as the Atlantic gale force wind tried its beat to pick us off and throw us far up the Sound of Mull. We drove across to the main road to Mallaig, which took us past the fish farm in Loch Ailot where salmon are harvested from large flat pontoons moored in the loch.

All the time and everywhere one went, the overriding impression was one of scale – of mountains and of seascapes, breathtaking and beautiful, unforgettable and addictive. I certainly was an addict returning year after year, and Kate was in the process of being converted. By Thursday evening she suggested that we went onto Mull for our last two days, and I had won. In a couple of hours the friendly manager, who was actually English, had sorted us out with a hotel for two nights on Mull at Glenforsa.

The next day we set off early and drove across the mountains to the ferry at Lochaline and quickly found our new hotel to be a Norwegian log cabin type of building with a rather attractive modern lounge overlooking the island's tiny aircraft landing strip.

Given only two days on Mull, what do you go to see? That was the problem. Tobermory of course was the first choice for that time of year. The peaceful little port with its clear waters hiding the wreck of a Spanish galleon is a rival to any Greek harbour – except for the weather. In the lengthening days of spring, the yachts were already beginning to arrive, dotting the bay with those graceful craft. By the time we'd wandered lazily around the bay and quaysides, there wasn't too much time to do anything else but drive slowly back to the hotel to prepare for dinner. It was Friday evening and the following day was to be our last of the holiday, so we sat in the lounge before dinner and planned what we would do on our last day. Duart Castle, home of Clan MacLean, was certainly on our list, and we began to argue what else we could do.

"Tim, look!" Kate pointed through the big picture windows at the tiny aircraft which was coming in to land just as dusk was taking hold.

I stood and watched as it rolled in along the strip and turned and came back to park not a hundred yards from the hotel. Only three people got out of it. I was just about to turn away commenting that business wasn't very brisk, when something vaguely familiar about one of the men caught my attention.

"Kate, come here!"

She came.

"Look. Is that figure familiar to you?"

"It's the professor, isn't it?"

"Yes, that's exactly who I think it is too." Now what on earth is *he* doing here? I wondered.

The trio from the aircraft made their way up to the hotel and into the reception area. The open staircase from the lounge went down into the foyer so we were able to see that one of the men was indeed Professor Stewart. We waited until he was busy at the reception desk before we wandered quietly down the stairs. The proprietor was just telling him that dinner would be ready in a few minutes when I concentrated and projected a greeting to him on a thought wavelength.

He straightened up as though he'd been shot and stared at the man in front of him. Our weeks of practising thought communications had certainly improved proficiency. I could feel the communication get through to him. This time it wasn't so woolly as it had been in Northallerton Church. Back came the echo only a little ragged around the edges.

"Are you all right, sir?" asked the man in Reception. The professor shook his head, slightly bemused now that he realised the greeting hadn't come from the man in front of him.

"Yes. . . yes, of course," he answered and at the same time turned. But he turned first to his left to look at his two companions before he looked across the rest of the foyer to where we were standing at the foot of the stairs, and then his eyes almost popped out and his mouth hung stupidly open for a second.

I walked across the foyer towards him.

His first words weren't as you might have expected - hello. Instead he closed his mouth and asked, "Was that you?"

I nodded as we shook hands and he put both hands to his head.

"Do it again."

He was almost rude in his request, but I could well understand it. He'd had quite a shock finding out that his own mind had the power of communication too. I did it again, but there was no answering communication as there always was with Kate. There was a great barrier there which was not allowing entry to full mind communication – not yet, anyway.

"I hear you, I really do," nodded Professor Stewart in great glee, "but what an earth are you two doing here? He turned to Kate rather belatedly and clasped her hand.

"Hello, Kate. I'm pleased to see you both of course, but I'll bet you're not so pleased to see me."

"What are you doing here, Professor?"

"I'm sorry, Kate, if I've stumbled accidentally on your honeymoon hotel, but you see I am from Mull originally and I quite often take a long weekend up here by flying in from Glasgow. I thought I'd fit one in before you two got back and we had our weekends occupied again."

Of course it fitted. I'd been surprised when I first heard his soft Scot's accent, but I'd never asked him where he'd come from originally.

"No, you've not really intruded on us." I explained where we'd been for most of the week in Ardnamurchan and why we were not on Mull.

"Look, Professor, if you don't get rid of that bag and have a wash you're going to miss dinner." The hotel was one of those where everyone sat down together at the same time, and they looked a bit askance at people coming in late. So he went off, while we finished our drinks.

The dinner gong had sounded and we and most other people were seated before the professor reappeared and went to sit down at another table until I waved him across to join us.

"But you'll be wanting privacy on your honeymoon."

Kate and I laughed at him and told him not to be so silly and to sit down. He didn't take much more persuading. He obviously was very pleased to see us, all the more since we went on at great length how much we liked Mull.

Eventually, as we approached the dessert course he asked, "If tomorrow is your last day, what have you got planned?"

"Actually we were just planning it when your plane came in and disturbed us," said Kate, "and we haven't got round to sorting it out yet. So far we are going to Duart Castle."

"Yes, that's one of the best places, but since you only have one day can I suggest—" He stopped and put both of his hands together pursing his lips.

"Yes. . . go on," urged Kate.

"The only thing is, it'll take you all day and you'll not have time to see Duart."

"Well, if it's worth doing, that doesn't matter. Where is it?"

"Why don't you go to Iona?"

"Of course," I said.

"Well, that's it settled then – Iona it is," Kate decided instantly and then she noticed the professor trying to suppress an air of sudden excitement, and instantly I closed down my mind communications. Too late, she noticed. She looked at each of us in turn.

"Tell me, Timothy Drummond, what have you and he hatched up between you?"

"Nothing, Kate. We've not even talked about it, honestly," I laughed.

"You *must* have. *He*. . ." she gestured to the professor, ". . .looks like the cat that got the cream. Something's cooking and I have the feeling that I won't like it."

Professor Stewart still never answered but continued trying to look as though he wasn't hatching anything.

Kate looked from one to the other of us, trying to look fierce in the dim light, but unfortunately for her she only managed to look more attractive than ever. Then the penny dropped.

"Iona is an old monastery, isn't it?" She nodded in understanding.

"It's older than old, Kate. It's *the* oldest in northern Britain."

"Ah, so I was right. I *knew* you wouldn't be able to keep quiet much longer."

"Yes, and I'm sorry, Kate, on your honeymoon. But it *is* a chance not to be missed, isn't it? It's not everyday that we can wander around Iona. Do you realise that St Columba came to Iona in AD 563? That is nearly another 800 years before Fountains and Rievaulx came into being. It has, therefore, been a place of virtually continuous worship for a very long time. It therefore fulfils the conditions for being a place of resonance attuned to Tim's gift. You cannot miss the chance, Kate. Look, it was meant to be, me being here at the same time as you. Pure chance, you might think, or was it destiny?"

Kate bowed her head, and when she looked up again she was smiling and she nodded. "Okay, okay, I give in. It's Iona tomorrow."

I wonder if she would have agreed so readily if she'd known what I was going to do.

The following morning we were up early again and on the road, heading for Fionnphort. We took the single-track road to Craigmure where the ferries from Oban landed, then on past Duart Castle (now to be left for a future visit), and on to the Pilgrims' Way, the Glenmore Road through the mountains. Running out of Glenmore, we passed the turn-off which would eventually take us back to Salen. We pressed on through Bunessan and Pennyghael. Eventually, some time later we reached Fionnphort just before twelve o'clock. At Fionnphort you have to leave the car and take the ferryboat to Iona. We'd obviously picked the right time of year for this visit. There were several boats moored against the slipway but no sign of a ferryman. While Professor Stewart wandered off looking for him, Kate and I stood on the slipway looking across the narrow channel to Iona.

We stood close looking to the low grey island with its cathedral. For fourteen hundred years Iona had been a focal point of this Christian world. By the seventh century Iona was the unquestioned centre of Christian teaching. To Iona, men from all parts of Europe came to meditate, to learn wisdom and Christianity and to return again to their own countries to continue the avalanche that had been Christianity. That particular avalanche had ceased to be an avalanche now; humanity was perhaps at or close to the point in time when it needed a new avalanche to begin, not necessarily a *new* faith but a *renewed* faith. Could Iona once again provide the means?

The professor returned with the ferryman, a little put out at having to make the crossing just before lunch. At that time the ferryboat was little more than a large cobble, which could hold about thirty people, I suppose. Despite that, it didn't corkscrew as much as the car ferry had done at Corran.

We walked up through the village and across to the cathedral. Past St Columba's tomb we entered the church and stood just inside. It was the first time that we had attempted this in a building which wasn't a ruin. The present church had in fact been a ruin until it had been given to the Church of Scotland by the eighth Duke of Argyll in 1899 and it had been rebuilt by the outbreak of the First World War.

As befits the cradle of Christianity in Britain, all Christian groups come to the Abbey. During the summer the Iona community arranges for people of all religions to come to Iona for a week of renewal of challenge and growth together. It was potentially, then, a very potent place in which we were now standing, for it still performed its function in the modern world. For some time we absorbed the peace emanating from the simplicity of the stark stone building until finally the professor broke the silence.

"Tim, we have to decide what you are going to do now. I think you ought to have a particular object in mind. We have a strong force here which you should take advantage of."

I nodded. I had already decided what I was going to try for. I put out one hand to Kate and felt her long slim sensitive fingers. She too knew what I wanted to do, and in all honesty she wasn't very keen on the idea. For the professor's sake we communicated on the voice level.

"Professor, at Mount Grace Priory something very powerful threw me down. I believe that it was another communications channel to... something... I don't know what. Perhaps it was God. Perhaps it was some other intermediate being or thing. Whatever it was, I have to have a go at communicating with it."

He nodded. We hadn't spoken about it on the way here, but nevertheless all three of us had known that this time it just had to be this one. We couldn't go on ignoring it forever.

"Can I suggest that the best place is likely to be outside the church on the little hillock which is reputed to be the site of St Columba's cell. It's probably *the* most potent spot and it's also grassy if you get thrown around again."

I agreed and we walked outside again. There were no other people around as we stood on Tor Abb facing the church.

This time Kate and I were already in full communication before we started to concentrate. The sort of mental handholding seemed to make it much easier, or perhaps it was just the power of this place. As the sub-brain opened up, the pathways in the mind seemed to glow with a power I'd not experienced before. The laser-like energy wave was fine and shining with a new energy, a latent power which I reached out for and touched, but I didn't know what I was to do with it. I was linked totally with Kate's mind too, and she was doing the same thing. This was the first time we'd compounded our joint brain power and it was truly awesome to try to visualise what we could do together. As I had a greater degree of practice, we concentrated on the one mind and looked for that highway that I'd touched momentarily at Mount Grace Priory.

For years I'd discussed religion and sought a truth. Now I was sure that I was within an ace of finding that truth and I was convinced that it would be nothing like we expected. Over the centuries the scaffolding of the Church had become so huge, so dense, that it wasn't possible to squeeze into the centre. Now the pathway was opening up. Ah! As I flashed through the levels I recognised the recognition pattern of the highway. I'd found it!

Or had I? Warily, carefully, fearfully, I put up maximum resistance to the communications path and made the connection. Yes, my goodness, it definitely *was* something new, something totally out of our previous concept, but it wasn't what I'd hoped for. It wasn't a communications channel to God or whatever. It was a communications channel to energy. Here was a powerhouse, able to create matter from energy and, conversely, create energy from matter simply by tapping, converting, and moulding energy from the equation that all physicists know: $E=mc^2$. Incredibly, it seemed that each one of us had his own little power converter lying stagnant in our hidden minds. Disappointed as I was at not finding what I'd hoped for and expected from this gate, it was necessary somehow to develop this power and to prove it out. We must be getting to the maximum usage of the brain by now, and it could be that Iona was the only place that this effect could be controlled. Very well, here goes. What could I do? Kate was growing very wary and worried now. We looked around momentarily in her mind too, but could find nothing comparable to this. Doubtless it was there somewhere and given time we could find and open it up. In the meantime I'd have to make do with mine. I was aware of Kate urging me to take care. And then I was aware of something else too. My upper brain suddenly fused as one with the lower sub-brain and the single highway between the two developed into a matrix of linking pathways under the action of the energy already overflowing from this new cavern. I was consciously able to manipulate my eyes and hands and could talk, much to Professor Stewart's astonishment. He was so surprised that he almost fell over as I described to him what was happening. Previously, of course, he'd had to rely on Kate's second-hand descriptions, but now he was getting it hot off the press.

I could feel that all I had to do was reach out with this power and move mountains. I wondered if I could. Not mountains of course, but something smaller. The professor had put down his haversack on the grass near his feet. I could detect the energy of the bag. It was composed, of course, mainly of space, as is the universe. But it had the semblance of solidity because atoms and molecules were held in a rigid structure by a force. Why hadn't I seen it before? By exerting my energy transfer field I was able to generate a transmission channel at the bag which released the force of structure, and use the energy wave to modulate a high energy transfer beam with the released atoms, and I transferred them some twenty metres away across the grass. Carefully I judged the height of the centre of gravity of the structure of the bag and allowed another few inches, then I released the transfer wave and collapsed the energy field. Instantly the bag and its contents reformed and dropped the two inches to the ground.

The professor's eyes were popping out from his head with sheer excitement and Kate was getting worked up too.

"Tim, that was fantastic." His accent was unquestionably Scots now.

"How big an item can you move like that?"

I looked about me. There was a wheelbarrow full of grass cuttings beside the church. Again I interpreted its molecular structure and assessed the power necessary to release its structural force long enough to transfer it at the speed of light to the gateway of the grounds. Yes, I could manage that, there didn't seem to be any limitation in sight here. Out of the atoms in my mind I conjured the transfer beam again and once again the barrow blinked out of existence by the side of the church and into position by the gate with hardly a blade of cut grass disturbed.

"Can you do that with yourself, Tim?"

"No." Kate wasn't willing for the experiment to go that far and she put up a strong resistance to the idea. But it did appeal to me and I had to know – we'd come too far now for turning back. For some minutes Kate and I had our first argument at a very high mental level. But finally she gave in. Very, very reluctantly she first of all conceded that I should examine the possibility of doing it. That of course was virtually agreement to proceed, for if I felt I could do it I was unlikely to back off.

"Be careful, Tim, it could be very dangerous." In the final moment of stress she reverted to plain language. Because of that it placed the emphasis more on the dangerous aspect of this part of the experiment. It could be that this was the reason that no sign remained of the mystics of the past – they had simply blinked out of existence, their atoms spread evenly around the universe.

"Okay, Professor, I'm going to give it a try. Look over there – St Martin's Cross just outside the church's doorway. That's where I'm going – I hope."

"Good luck, Tim. If you really feel in danger don't hesitate to abort." I don't know how he expected me to abort in the middle of taking an atomic structure apart.

I looked very carefully at my own 'solid' structure. One of the characteristics of a solid is that the molecules are close together, but this is only very relatively speaking. There is still more space there than solid. The molecules in a solid matrix are held fixed and vibrate around a fixed position in a regular way, thus giving the solid its fixed state. In a liquid they are very slightly further apart and vibrate more rapidly for short distances in no regular pattern, thus allowing a liquid to flow. In a gas the separation is much wider and the molecules move at high speed in all directions, colliding with each other, and as a result they fill as much space as they are allowed. In converting a solid to a liquid and then to a gas, energy is added normally in the form of heat.

The process of breaking down a solid for transmission was in fact accomplished by passing it through these three phases almost instantaneously by the injection of energy derived from the space around. From the high energy gas phase there was then a third transposition to a fourth phase from gas to pure energy, as Einstein had foreseen in his Theory of Relativity when he declared that mass and energy are really no more than the same thing in different forms. This, at that time, was a flat contradiction of two of the classical laws. The first was the conservation of matter which laid down that though matter could be turned into different forms of matters, none could be taken away or added. The second was the conservation of energy saying something very similar about energy, but the total amounts of each in the universe remained the same. Einstein was proved correct, and the classical laws wrong, with the explosion of the first atomic bomb. Now I had found another simpler less-destructive controlled conversion process by sheer manipulation of the mind.

To break down and restructure an object was relatively easy because I had total control of the high energy transfer beam all the time myself and was able to reform the object in the new place from the pattern temporarily stored in my mind. To do it with oneself was much more difficult because the transfer beam needed to carry much more information. The molecular pattern and structure needed to be imprinted on the wave and in split-second timing, transmitted like a holograph with the total pattern of information present on the whole beam in the instant before the modulating energy wave is driven up to full power for molecular breakdown and conversion.

Very, very carefully I set up the intricate molecular structure pattern and directed it onto the transfer beam aimed at a point near St Martin's Cross with the centre of gravity of the solid pattern sufficiently high for the bottom of the pattern to be several inches above the ground.

Already the molecular pattern was set in its new position when I momentarily took time to communicate to Kate that I was on my way. There was little response, only an overwhelming sense of caring and concern.

The moment had arrived. I had only to extract from the space around me the energy required to give three changes of phase in an instant. As I wound up to the energy level required, it was like charging a battery preparatory to flashing off. Just in the instant before release I subconsciously, or perhaps more correctly sub-subconsciously, was aware, down amongst the densest part of the neuron structure, that yet another brain area was responding to a previously undetected signal modulation. A signal modulation which was transmitted by pure white energy itself. But it was too late to analyse this. I released the energy and. . . and how do you describe a split second of *nothing* – the time it takes to travel a hundred metres at the speed of light? And yet time itself is relative, as the great Einstein also calculated. But he never predicted anything like this. For what seemed an age I existed as a sheer beam of energy with information that was me keyed into it in the form of a modulating signal. In reality I flashed out of existence on the hillock by the professor and flashed into existence exactly at the predicted spot. As my molecular pattern reformed and I controlled the incoming transfer beam, I realised that I'd made a mistake. I'd forgotten that all speed is relative. Nothing in the universe is fixed. I'd forgotten the Earth's spin and the motion round the sun. With the bag I'd automatically corrected during the reforming process, but with myself everything had to be spot on in the transmission phase. The distance, and hence the time involved, was infinitesimal, but the difference in relative velocities caused by that lapse was sufficient to give me a speed relative to the ground as I rematerialised. What was more important, I had a speed relative to St Martin's Cross. I should have picked any other spot to rematerialise, but it was too late as I realised my error.

The result anywhere else on the grass would have been a bad fall. The result here was that a second after materialising at speed I dropped the inch to the ground and ran full tilt at speed straight into the stone cross.

The result of this was predictable – I knocked myself out. As my motor systems closed down from the shock, they put out a total all-systems-shut-down which could not be ignored, and I blacked out – totally - again.

Chapter Sixteen
The Final Communion

Once again I came to, to find myself in a hospital. It really was becoming a habit. As I became conscious, slowly clawing my way out of an infinite blackness, I was aware of a total body ache as though I'd been used extensively as a punch bag! The aches and pains were screaming along thousands of nerveways from the tips of my toes to the top of my head. They all carried one overpowering message - pain. As I groaned at the sheer force of it all, I opened my eyes and the memory flooded back. I remembered the great flood of energy and the matrix of highways between the upper and lower brain which had been opened up, and I cast around looking for them but the matrix had disappeared. There were, however, a few more constricted pathways open which materially affected my mental facilities. I could remember quite clearly what had happened.

My eyes cast around the room and came to rest on a familiar figure - Kate - in an armchair near the bed. She was asleep with a worried frown spoiling the tranquillity of her face. I felt the exclamation rise into my mind, and almost automatically the call was transferred and transmitted on our private communications channel. At the last minute I tried to stop it as I realised that she probably needed the sleep badly. But it was too late and in an instant she was awake and across to my bedside as her internal communications system received the call.

"Tim, thank goodness. How are you feeling?" She pressed a button on the wall before gingerly taking hold of my hands.

"I feel like I've had an argument with a double Decker bus. What's the damage this time?"

"It wasn't a double-decker bus, Tim, it was a cross."

"Oh yes, I remember what happened well enough."

"Do you. . .?" There was some relief mixed with the question.

". . .you've got a broken nose, a broken arm and a fractured leg, together with a great deal of bruising. What went wrong, Tim?"
"It was stupid really. Next time I'll get—"
"Next time?" There was a chill in the question. "Tim, after this there *isn't* going to be a next time."
"But, Kate, there has to be. I can't leave it there now, can I?"
"But it's dangerous, Tim."
"Not if I do it properly."
"But why didn't you—"
"Now come along, you two. You're not fighting already, are ye?"

Judging by the accent of the nurse who had just arrived in response to the button call, I was still in Scotland. I went through all the rituals of temperature, pulse, blood pressure, etc., and she gave me an injection. It wasn't until I was slipping into an unconscious state again, this time drug induced, that I thought to ask and only just managed to set it out: "How long have I been unconscious?"

"Oh, only two days this time," was Kate's answer, together with something else which I heard but didn't take in as I once again lost contact with the present for a time.

The next time I recovered my senses the pain levels were vastly reduced and bearable this time.

The professor had again disappeared back to Sheffield to work, with a promise to come back north to drive us home when the hospital would let me go. By tacit mutual agreement we never talked about what had happened the whole time that I was in the hospital. Each day for nearly a fortnight Kate came in to stay with me for two visits a day. After the first week, with a plaster cast on my arm and another on my leg, I was allowed up for the first time, and by the Thursday of the following week the doctor said that he would let me out on Sunday. It was my left arm that was broken and my right leg, so with a bit of practice with a stick I could just about hobble around by the Sunday lunchtime when Professor Stewart arrived to chauffeur us home. I had apparently missed the time of my life. I'd been lifted out of Iona by helicopter to hospital in Oban, so we had quite a drive to do to get home in the daytime. All the hospital staff had been bursting with curiosity as to what had happened to me, but here the protective arm of government had fallen. It was they who at the professor's urgent request had provided the RAF helicopter and the private guarded room in the hospital.

As usual, the professor started out the drive with the best of intentions, showing all concern for my welfare, but really as eager as ever to discuss what had happened, and very soon it broke through. It took a little longer this time, as he had been rather shaken at what had happened.

"Why did it go wrong, Tim?"

So I told him all about the problem of relative speeds which he grasped immediately.

"So next time you'll get it right?"

"Yes, I think so,"

"You *think* so?" Kate was quickly onto the implied doubt.

"You have to be more sure than thinking before I'll let you do that again, Tim Drummond."

I tried to think of another topic to head her off and I had a sudden thought.

"I meant to ask you, Kate. We were in full communication until the actual material dissolution and transfer. What did it feel like to you?"

She realised that I was putting her off, but answered nevertheless.

"Well, you know what it's like to be fully merged, acting virtually as one brain. I was able to follow all you were doing up to the point when you started to increase the energy content and the interference became very heavy until I had to start shielding it out, so I had to withdraw from that area of the brain and follow it sort of second-hand through your high-level conscious area. Then, at the point you disappeared, my mind went empty. It was like leaning on something and then having it pulled away suddenly. I sort of mentally toppled over. When I re-established my equilibrium, you were doing your best to push the stone cross over, and before I could re-establish contact, you'd blacked out, and all I could find were routine housekeeping operations taking place. You'd gone."

"That's still the interesting question, isn't it, Kate? Which part is me and where had I gone? In fact, where did I go when I turned my material body into energy for that instant?"

"That could be the answer to it all, you know," said the professor. "Perhaps the ultimate answer is that *you* are energy?"

"*Intelligent* energy?"

"Why not?"

"Mmm," I mused, and then I remembered something else and drew a sharp breath.

Kate's hearing was attuned well. "What is it, Tim?"

"It's nothing."

"Yes, it is. I want to know. You're cooking something up again, aren't you?"

So I explained about the moment of near peak energy conversion when I'd detected another modulated signal on the energy wave itself.

"So it goes on and on." Kate put her head in her hands. As I looked at her and wished I could put my plastered arm around her, I felt another kind of pain. In the old days it would have been described as a heartache, but I knew that such feelings emanated from the brain *not* the heart. For the moment the professor wasn't saying anything. He contented himself with negotiating the highland roads, waiting, biding his time to see what the decision would be.

There was no doubt that he would opt to go on. He was a scientist, and though we might be very close friends by now, he would expect me to investigate every new phenomenon which came up. He'd thought that we were at the ultimate pitch on Iona and that was our limit until the avalanche effect took a hold. Now there was at least one more step to aspire to first.

Eventually Kate took her hands away and simply said, "But you'll wait until you are better again, won't you?" Her soul searching had reached the same conclusion as mine. This thing was obviously dangerous if it was slightly mishandled. But the human race had not got where it was now by shirking danger.

"What do you think it was, Tim?" The decision made for him, Professor Stewart came back into the conversation.

"I think, or hope, it was what I thought this energy thing was when I first came across it – a superintelligence."

He nodded quietly and we drove on in silence for a while. Kate broke the silence in the end.

"The Bible says that God spoke to Adam and Eve. Do you think that that story is a strong race memory of a time when this facility that Tim has was in common use, communicating with a being or beings outside this world? The fall from grace could be all that was left of some tremendous calamity which sealed us off from those powers of communication and energy conversion and remembrance."

It was certainly a possibility. I looked out at the majesty of the mountainous countryside through which we were passing and thought about that oft-spoken phrase: "Faith can move mountains". That now seemed a possibility in itself. It was still a task too large for my one single mind, but for a group mind it was possible. Extrapolate that to holding a world in orbit around a sun, or a sun in its position in the Galaxy, or a Galaxy in its position in the universe. Was that possible for a joint, conscious, intelligent energy entity? Was that God – our ideas of God are really too simple for a universe as complex as ours. The concept was mind-stretching, and somewhere along the line I usually lost it even with my expanded brain capacity. This capacity had certainly been enlarged now. I had no trouble in finding information from the past for which the professor had compiled his neat information storage gene theory. Iona seemed to have broadened this out for me, broken down barriers, and laid out roads and tunnels which had only been paths previously. It added several dimensions to a thought and heightened ordinary thinking. Although I had tried several times I had not been able to restore contact with the energy generator. It and the vast expanding matrix of paths between the conscious and sub-brain which it had generated were for the time lost again. The vast matrix was essential to enable instant computation of the large amount of data that was required. I could only hope that in the weeks to come I would be able to re-establish it at a suitable focus point.

We talked a lot on that trip south. We talked of each other and our friends, we philosophised about the object of life and what the human race had achieved and could achieve as it stood now, of the likely effects of this superbrain capability being applied on a large scale – but regularly we came back to this one more thing that we had to do and when and where we would do it.

By the time we reached home we had come to no conclusions as to where it should be done. We thought that given some luck we could try in four weeks time. That would be on the 29th March, but we decided that it would be more suitable on 1st May – Monday, 1st May.

From then on, all our thoughts were directed to 1st May. I didn't allow myself to think of anything, and after that we lived for the days. One by one they arrived and departed. I continued with this account of our experiences and fought it onto paper. Some days I couldn't find the words to write and other days they came in a great flood of feeling.

After two weeks I managed to get back to work, complete with plasters, but it was good to be working again. I had to hold in my relative powers and try to only use my normal brain level at work to prevent awkward questions being asked. Bob Atwell was highly inquisitive of course and he wanted to know everything that had happened down to the last detail, which was very nearly the conversion of the last material molecule into energy. He listened with a red face and in total awe as I described the energy converter, and he became one of the group waiting for the 1st May to arrive.

Frank Cooper too had telephoned several times, but he had Eileen ill in bed and so couldn't get down to see me. I was sorry about that.

Slowly but surely, the days ticked by and we finally arrived at the last weekend in March. The professor duly arrived on our doorstep on the Saturday evening, ready to take the decision as to where it should be done. Bob Atwell wasn't missing out on this one and had promised to telephone on Sunday to find out where we'd decided on.

We kept off the subject until we'd had dinner.

"Where is it to be then, Jim?"

"First of all, are you feeling fit enough, Tim?"

I drew breath to answer.

"Yes, he is." Kate answered for me. She smoothed back her golden hair from her forehead in a nervous gesture which had become more noticeable in the past few days.

"He's got his leg plaster off, his nose is more or less okay, his bruises have gone, and the hospital put a clean new plaster on his arm yesterday. We can't bear the tension anymore. It has to be Monday."

The professor looked at me and I merely nodded. She was right, the tension was building now and could only find release in one way.

"I haven't decided where, Tim. I know that the last time I felt that we shouldn't go to Thornborough again, but it was the most—"

"No, not Thornborough, it's too distracting historically. It has to be Mount Grace. I've called in there three times this week in preparation and—"

"So that's why you've been late, and I thought you were working."

"Sorry, Kate, I didn't tell you. I didn't want you to worry. As I said, I went there to see if I can still locate that energy gate. It was there, you'll remember, that I got the first bolt from it."

"And did you find it?" Jim Stewart quietly prompted me. I looked from one to the other.

"I did, yes. On the second night I found it, but I didn't connect with it."

"And on the third night?" It was Kate's turn to quietly prompt me.

"On the third night I found it immediately. Practice, it would seem, makes perfect. But no, I haven't connected to it still. I promised to wait until Monday and that's what we'll do, but it has to be Mount Grace, Professor. No doubt about it."

And Mount Grace it was. Monday 1st May – May Day. The year was moving on and it was already a warm day when we arrived at Mount Grace Priory at ten in the morning. We chose an early time to avoid the day-trippers who would flood in to the place after lunch. There were only a few couples wandering about at this time and it was easy enough for us to avoid them.

We chose the same little garden cloister as previously, except that this time we all crammed into it.

"Are you ready, Tim?" the professor asked, as though he was on a field study.

I nodded. "In a moment we will be." Kate and I opened up our communications channel to each other and flooded across into each other's mind in a wild embrace of thought. Jointly, we reached out to the professor and after a moment's pause our joint power reached him and he smiled, a rare smile of total pleasure. As yet, he wasn't able to respond, but he knew that it would come. For the moment he was content to know that he was getting a joint first-hand account of the state of play. Not satisfied yet, we reached out again. This experiment was so important that I felt that a wordy description would be useless. Bob Atwell deserved as complete a picture as the professor. As we activated his receiver and transmitted total reassurance, he got over his shock at the sudden expansion in his mind and was content to wait. We must have made an odd group to anyone watching. Three men and a tall golden-haired girl, grouped in a little square of garden, in our own little square of thought (or perhaps if we'd held hands it would have been a circle). As I achieved an inner peace I shortly felt Kate achieve the same level. Our joint peace reached out to the professor and Bob. The professor stopped fiddling with a lump of stick he'd picked up, and Bob lost his nervous smile and his red face faded to a normal healthy pink. Up to this point you could say that we had all been conducting a joint mind-soothing, peace therapy. From that moment things became much more serious.

Mount Grace hadn't quite the potency of Iona, and it is doubtful whether if I hadn't been to Iona I could have achieved the depth of feeling necessary. However, the barriers had been largely dissipated at Iona and I knew the way. I had the key to the intervening bulkheads and it only needed the resonance of Mount Grace's past glories to turn it. The code was broken and the tumblers fell apart and the way was cleared into the sub-brain. I avoided the routes to the memory banks. They were precious too, but today there was more at stake than the past. Once again, the future of mankind beckoned. Together, Kate and I rode the laser-like total energy beam. No longer did it throb or oscillate uncertainly. It was almost perfectly tuned to a pitch of resonance. I felt the professor and Bob Atwell draw their breaths, totally aghast at our wordless transmitted description of this force. For the first time they really realised what this was all about. Wordy descriptions had prepared them, but only very inadequately, for this kaleidoscopic of mental powers, this display of superhuman power. The highways of the mind were all all right and glowing and there was a total synchronisation of thought as the energy level rose and rose. I found the gate and made the connection.

The communications system became part of the energy conversion system, and as previously the upper and lower brains fused into a complex matrix of paths criss-crossing all the barriers. The energy, now tapped into, swept all the debris of the mind away, and at last the whole of the brain was in use - a powerhouse of thought. I even thought that the fourth dimension, that of time, was breachable. That indeed would be an interesting thought to follow - but not yet. The flashing molecules, atoms, electrons and ions created a mini universe of ordered thought. For a moment I savoured the feeling, but then drove on and escalated the power available. As the accumulator charged up, as though ready for a material transfer, I established the transfer beam and escalated further. Atomic structure dissolved and in a controlled expansion I converted to hold the waves. In all directions it radiated out and then, as it passed the critical point where transmission of matter was possible, it began to hum to an externally imposed wave pattern. At this point on Iona I had released the pent-up energy and physically moved, but this time I held it, searching for the meaning of the signal. I increased the power even further and the modulation came in very strongly. Undoubtedly it was intelligent. It communicated on a high-level energy beam used no doubt to punch its way through the universe.

The signal I decoded off the energy transfer beam and onto my normal communications network and thence onto my normal upper brain for decoding into intelligible thought. Hooked into this level of thought were Professor Stewart and Bob Atwell, and of course Kate. Kate had stopped at the gate leading to the fiery furnaces where thought and energy merged into one. She wasn't ready yet to travel this far. As she waited there monitoring the signals from the heavens, she and the others caught the first interpretation of a cosmic intelligence. It interpreted into a vast infinite well of knowledge and power, beyond even my super-energised brain's comprehension. As we waited without breathing (for breathing was no longer necessary as time stood still), the being sending the communication transmitted a picture of infinity, of worlds and of suns orbiting in vast patterns of matter and antimatter. Across the voids of the physical universe and other universes in thousands of dimensions and times it stretched its tendrils of energy to communicate with all intelligence that could or would hold communication with it. Nothing was too big or too small. From the giant suns of the Milky Way to the repeated patterns of even the timeless crystalline rocks, the universe abounded with intelligence. Worlds within worlds, universes within universes, the cacophony of intelligent communication was absorbed, directed, and redirected and distributed by... by what? Was this now the God of my childhood, the bearded Israelite standing by the tree playing with the children and the birds? Was this the reason behind Christianity, behind the other faiths of our world? The only dimly-imagined, never seen presence? Were we then standing at the gates of heaven? Was heaven the merging of oneself? One's real self, that is, that ethereal never-to-be-discovered real self that is you, with this greater all-permeating intelligence. Was the *me* that is me a concept based on energy?

If this was heaven, then where or what was hell? After a contact like this, hell could only be the absence of this. The answers to all these questions lay only a little infinity further on. As yet, the entity was only sending out universal signals which I was receiving and interpreting. There remained the final step forward. By a slight increase in my own energy level I would be able to send a message to which it would respond.

For too long the human race had not had this type of communication, and I wasn't sure that I'd be able to stand up to the fierce energy content that a direct absorption into the total mental entity would mean. Time, as I said, had stopped, and Professor Stewart and Bob Atwell were frozen in an overwhelming emotional collapse. Kate held onto me tenuously. We held hands physically, tightly; long slender and sensitive, her fingers entwined tightly with mine; her eyes, framed in the golden light reflecting from the sun, were bathed in tears as for a brief moment of eternity I hesitated. I was like a bridge between the physical world and the profound intelligence of energy. I didn't really have a choice. Kate knew that and I knew it too. Even as I stepped up the energy conversion in my transfer wave, Kate and I were consumed in a mental embrace at the highest and deepest level.

My signal was put out at an energy level previously unachieved. A call from the human race to its destiny.

Perhaps after all, I could survive it and the knowledge so returned would offer man his place in the kingdom of the universe. At a speed unrestricted by light my communication travelled out through all the dimensions of space and time. Undetectable by the great radio telescopes of our own technology, it travelled on a waveband unused from the planet Earth since the Fall of Adam.

The response was immediate. That particular word, of itself, implies time, but there was no time gap. The entity directed a joyous surge of energy along one of its many paths across the known cosmos. Faster than light – it *was* possible after all – came the reply, through the whirling vortices of space, along the Milky Way to find the source of that single cry from a lost but not forgotten planet.

As a father clutches at a lost child, the being that all the human race who believe calls God reached out and clasped in a tremendous outpouring of joy and welcome. Even as he reached out I knew that the energy differentials were too great and I knew that Kate knew this too, and as my all too human brain, so recently discovered, began to disintegrate under the powerful energy surge, I knew too that I wasn't losing Kate either. As we began to disentangle our joint mind I knew that she too now knew the way.

Chapter Seventeen
Postscript

A week after the cataclysmic events of May Day, I knelt in the tiny village churchyard behind the church. Alone at last, I knelt in the freshly cut grass in front of the newly turned earth that was Tim Drummond's grave. His last wish as his spirit left me alone had been for his human body to be buried in the churchyard in his village.

The professor had had a post-mortem done before Tim had been buried, and his brain had been found to be fused hard – visible evidence of that power which I'd stood on the side lines and watched. I'd finished Tim's story off for him of course, as I was the only one who'd been close enough in his mind to see that last awesome crack in time when Tim had called out with such clarity and certainty to his God. But he'd called out to me as well, and I knew that somewhere, sometime, Tim and I would join our minds and spirits again.

Only Professor Stewart and Bob Atwell knew why I was so happy for Tim. Poor old Frank Cooper had missed out on the experience of a lifetime, but between us the experimentation would continue. The avalanche had begun. The professor's old brain in his lecture theatre had started something which would take the human race back into the mainstream of life. The professor would see to that. He and Bob Atwell were already on their way to stand in the centre of the circle at Thornborough. Doubtless the time would come when we would all again stand on Iona and reach out, searching for Tim's spirit.

Before he'd left I'd confided in Jim Stewart the one thing that no one else yet could know. It wasn't actual confirmed knowledge yet even for myself, but nevertheless I knew it for a fact. It wasn't just any child that Tim and I had conceived. Our seeds of history, of knowledge of time and of the future had been combined together. What sort of human he would be I had no idea, but Professor Stewart had already chosen his name. After all, Tim's godfather had no other choice to make.

Men, my brothers, men the workers ever reaping something new:
That which they have done but earnest of the things that they shall do:
For I dipt into the future, far as human eye could see,
Saw the vision of the world, and all the wonders that would be.
Heard the heavens filled with shouting, and there rained a ghastly dew.
From the nations' airy navies grappling in the central blue.
In the Parliament of man, the Federation of the World.
Science moves but slowly, slowly creeping on from point to point.
Yet I doubt not thro' the ages one increasing purpose runs.
And the thoughts of man are widen'd with the Process of the suns.
Knowledge comes, but wisdom lingers.

Alfred Lord Tennyson
1809–1892